THE LAST ARCADIAN

PART ONE

Z.S. JOSEPH

THE LAST ARCADIAN : Part One

Book Cover by Parker Nugent.

First Edition 2024

ISBN 979-8-9912914-9-1 (eBook)

ISBN 979-8-9912914-6-0 (pbk.)

PROLOGUE

Since the year 2000, scientists have identified and documented tens of thousands of near-Earth asteroids. While most of the asteroids found weren't an immediate threat to mankind, experts maintained that many more had not been discovered. As time went on, the potential for an asteroid affecting the Earth increased. In response, scientists across the world joined forces to safeguard humanity against the risks of a potential direct hit. Despite their best efforts, they could not prevent what would eventually come to pass: The Collision. A catastrophic, cosmic event where multiple asteroids crashed into the Earth, nearly wiping out all human existence.

Humanity was at first unable to cope with the destruction left in The Collision's wake; the survivors facing tremendous obstacles in their efforts to rebuild after the devastation caused by its impact. It would take many generations for the survivors of Earth to realize that the Collision brought both tragedy and a remarkable gift: Chrysalix. An unknown element scattered about the Earth in the Collision's wake. This element not only transformed the land, sea, and air, but also unlocked humanity's inherent ability to control space and time itself.

Humankind, once on the brink of total extinction, rapidly developed newfound abilities and flourished. New tribes formed, each possessing unique talents, which enabled them to manipulate space and time in a multitude of ways. As time went on, the tribes came together, forming alliances that transformed into factions. Eventually, the factions turned into nation-states, joining forces to create a new world government. This new order governed over the people of Earth and its Past, Present, and potential futures. To ensure the survival of humanity, the people of Earth embraced their new and powerful leaders with open arms: The Arcadians.

Under Arcadian rule, humanity joined forces, unified by a collective purpose. Their goal: unlock and harness the full power of Chrysalix and safeguard the Earth and Timeline from potential threats. Motivated by a renewed sense of purpose, mankind uncovered and honed new and extraordinary abilities. Their innovations brought about unprecedented advancements in spirituality and science.

Spiritual growth and technological advancements were rapid and plentiful, but would come at great cost. Humanity, inherently hungry for knowledge and power, eventually forgot about its troubled past. Once teetering on the edge of extinction, mankind tore itself into two camps: one based on religious dogma, and the other on scientific truth. The clash of ideologies pushed civilization to a tipping point, leading to a rebellion against their Arcadian rulers. A long and volatile war emerged, eventually resulting in the Arcadian's complete and total annihilation.

Humanity was quick to celebrate the fall of the Arcadians. However, they would just as soon discover that the demise of the world's greatest empire was not without consequences. After the fog of the war had lifted, leaders of the new world government uncovered a shocking revelation. The eradication of the Arcadians had diminished one of their most sacred abilities: the power to see into Earth's potential futures. Losing this ability left humanity exposed to future threats. Desperate to find a solution, the people of Earth sought comfort in their ideologies. Once again, humanity divided itself and cast aside its troubled history, struggling to maintain its survival.

Many years later, a standard mission to the Past–Before Collision–would uncover a groundbreaking discovery: the survival of the Arcadian bloodline. Humanity's leaders, no longer bound by a singular goal but split in their ideologies, would be swift to cast judgment. Their response to this revelation would set them down an alternative course. One that would either lead to humanity's long-term survival...or its swift and utter destruction.

Table of Contents

I.

ARRIVAL

It was the dead of night on a secluded dirt road in the countryside. The atmosphere was the same as always–dark and unnervingly tranquil. Nothing but the sound of wind whispering through the trees disturbed the otherwise complete silence. There was no sign of life anywhere to be found. No sense of liveliness. In fact, the road had been known to remain mostly undisturbed throughout the night. Those who took up residences anywhere one might consider 'nearby' were markedly reserved and austere, choosing to spend the evening hours with their families or in seclusion, with the latter hours being spent asleep soundly in quaint farmsteads scattered across the vastness of the countryside. The notable absence of artificial light added to the haunting appeal of the road, accompanied by a sky overflowing with scintillating stars that would mesmerize even the least observant passersby.

Any other time, on any other night, those familiar with the area would have considered it a perfectly pleasant evening. But from that point forward, it would be more appropriate to remember it as the calm before the storm. Upon that same country road, surrounded by dense trees on either side, two figures disturbed the peace, blinking into existence as though born of the air itself. Both appeared unconscious and gravely injured. Any coroner worth their salt would presume them dead at first glance–their bodies unmoving, clothes tattered and dusted in soot, arms and legs twisted and thrown about in unimaginable directions.

The first figure, a trim woman suited in leather armor so dark it faded into the backdrop of night, slowly regained consciousness. Struggling to regain her vision, she eventually came to. She struggled to identify any distinct images at first– only blurred, shadowy figures, as though she had opened her eyes underwater. To make matters worse, her unruly hair further obstructed her already fuzzy view. She brushed it away, helping her eyes to adjust, and as she did so, she breathed a momentary sigh of relief. Down the road, she spotted the silhouette of the second figure–a scruffy child, sprawled and unmoving amongst the dirt and rocks, draped in ragged clothes.

While the woman stammered to her feet, her short-lived respite was disturbed as two headlights rose over a nearby hill, closing in at an upsetting pace. Rather than succumb to panic, the woman clenched her fists, summoned her remaining strength, and willed herself to Jump to the child–a move she had enacted many times before that would transport her to the child in an instant, enabling her to usher the two of them swiftly out of harm's way.

Much to the woman's surprise, she remained motionless. *Why am I still here,* she thought, *when I should be there?* She tried again. Then a third time. Her sensibility was at once replaced by confusion and panic. She froze–an unmoving effigy in the darkness.

Move, she thought, *just...move.*

The woman hobbled desperately towards the middle of the road. With each pitiful step, waves of pain sent shockwaves up her spine. She cried out in frustration–and pain, and guilt, and suffering–still attempting to Jump in the child's direction. The distant headlights, drawing nearer, closed in on their position. She shunted her fear aside; her instincts triggered by the roars of the engine screaming towards the child. The woman's pace doubled, her heartbeat mirroring each feeble step, racing against time as the vehicle barreled towards the motionless child.

The woman neared the child as the automobile loomed ahead. She moved more quickly, desperate to close in. With a fleeting moment, in what was sure to be her final act, the woman flung herself over the child, squeezing tightly as she prepared herself for the coming calamity. Clenching her eyes, she extended a free arm out in a final, hopeless attempt to stop the car from unavoidable impact.

A cacophony of sounds met the woman's worried ears. The car's horn blared; the driver swerved; a series of horrendous screeches began bellowing into the night sky.

The car skid back and forth, kicking up debris that pelted the woman's wincing face. While clinging to the child, the chaotic whirlwind finally made its way past her. She turned back quickly and opened her eyes, spotting the vehicle in a bout with the road itself, fighting to regain control.

It doesn't.

The woman stares on, watching as the vehicle makes a final desperate swerve before catching an edge and tumbling through the air towards the side of a mountainous willow tree stemming from a roadside ditch. The truck falls to the ground, its nose diving into the trunk of the tree, bringing it to a sudden and horrifying stop.

Momentary peace and silence fill the air.

The silence is broken only by the sound of the overturned truck's horn thundering helplessly into the night.

2.

THE WANTING AND UNWONTED

Addy was in a deep sleep. Atop a quaint, wooden four post bed, and sunk amongst a sea of woolen blankets, she snored away soundly, both cozy and content. It was therefore no surprise that she was blind to the fact that a beast with jet-black fur had silently crept its way across Addy's room, to the top of her bed, and was now towering over her, staring intimately at her unmoving face.

Ever so slowly, the beast bent his head towards Addy's and placed an oversized paw squarely on her forehead.

Addy's eyes widened, connecting with those of the wolf-like creature above her.

The beast took immediate notice and started his attack.

"Good boy, Mico...thanks, boy," said Addy, making out words of appreciation between the onslaught of licks she received from Mico's coarse tongue while she scratched behind his ears. "Thanks, Mico...okay...good dog...thank you."

Satisfied with his work, Mico halted his loving assault, staring intensely at Addy through his distinctly colored eyes—one blue and one green, the same as his master. Panting with excitement, he motioned towards Addy, ready to commence another round of licking. Before he could reach her, he became distracted by the faint sound of a door opening and closing from the confines of the nearest room. Standing on guard and opting to investigate further, Mico hopped down from the bed and bound his way through a crack in the doorway, making a swift exit.

Wide awake, Addy pushed herself up, propping her back against a sea of pillows and the bed's oak headboard. Stretching her arms outwards to the ceiling, she recalled bits and pieces from another night of strange dreams. While she recalled having dreamt regularly before, the frequency and vividness of her dreams had escalated over the past few months. Most had included her best friend Eli and his brother Luka, which was ordinary enough. The strangeness revolved around the *setting* of her dreams–an unfamiliar and fluorescent planet, the inhabitants of which held strange abilities that she recounted as being akin to witches and wizards. Perhaps most oddly of all, the inhabitants of her dreams were not profoundly interested in her, but rather abrupt in their approach of intense questioning as to the whereabouts of her parents. Having never had the fortune of meeting them, Addy was often at a loss for words under such circumstances. What little she knew of them she learned only from her grandmother, Prue, who shared that, by all accounts, her parents were heroes, both having laid down their lives in the servitude of their country.

Despite her grandmother's effective storytelling abilities, the extent of her parent's described heroism seemed to come with some major plot holes. Not that of their personal sacrifice, which was admirable, but the nature of their circumstances and the feats they were said to perform before their demise. As a child, Prue would often tell stories to Addy about her parents–how her father had been a prince and her mother his destined princess. The two supposedly ruled over a kingdom as though by the will of magic itself and had lived happily ever after. Of course, as Addy became older, she eventually came to question the story's ending. For instance, how could they have lived in such bliss if they weren't able to live their days in peace and harmony together as a family?

Eventually, when Prue deemed her granddaughter old enough, she told Addy the truth–that she was adopted. Quite the revelation, Addy admitted, but one that she found rather obvious, if only due to the glaring difference in their accents. Prue was also quick to add that, despite her being adopted, she loved Addy with all her heart–a feeling that Addy never questioned and that she returned in kind. Over time, Prue would come to share everything that she knew about Addy's parentage, bringing an end to the fantastic façade she had built around her; though Addy still felt that Prue had likely embellished the truth here and there to comfort her granddaughter.

"Must be Gran's stories," surmised Addy, brushing away her thoughts. Then, in one swift motion, she threw her covers aside, jumped from the bed, made her way through the door, and capered across the hall into the bathroom.

Addy stood in front of the bathroom mirror. Letting the faucet run, she splashed herself in the face with icy water, awakening her instantly. She leaned forward, observing her reflection, looking past her pale complexion to her dark and rusty hair. While normally long and stunning, her locks were in a state of dishevelment, caused no doubt by her brief stints of tossing and turning throughout the night.

Putting her hair back, she looked into her own mismatched eyes and paused. *Had they become a shade darker overnight? And was such a thing even possible?* She had never heard of her condition–heterochromia, or as Prue put it, 'being far too lovely to be represented by a single color'–becoming even more extreme. She leaned forward, meticulously studying each iris, fixating on the mirror in hypnotic observation. Addy intensified her focus, concentrating on her eyes so much so that she barely noticed that her body temperature had elevated at an alarming rate, fogging up the mirrored glass before her.

"Adelynne!"

Addy's grandmother, Prue, joyfully yelled from behind her. She crept up silently, taking Addy by surprise. Addy jumped in fright, hitting her head in the mirror. Mico, standing at Prue's feet, stared up at his master, wagging his tail in excitement.

"Gran! Oh my God—you scared me," replied Addy, rubbing her forehead.

"I'm so sorry, my darling. I noticed you were up, and I simply couldn't wait any longer," said Prue, hugging Addy tightly and kissing her on each cheek. "Oh my, you're quite warm!" exclaimed Prue. "Anyway," she continued, quick to change the subject, "Happy Birthday, my dear. Now, get yourself washed up and come to the kitchen when you're ready. I've made your favorite breakfast!"

"Thanks Gran. Be there in a minute," said Addy, still distracted by her own thoughts.

Prue smiled and gave her granddaughter another kiss on the cheek. She took a step back, looked at Addy proudly, then turned and strutted off to the kitchen, Mico trailing happily behind her.

Addy faced back towards the mirror and wiped away the fog. Rather than continuing to focus on vain concerns such as the state of her eye color, she popped a blue contact into her green eye—though she now felt that one eye was a more pronounced shade of blue—undressed and stepped into the shower.

Feeling revitalized, Addy returned to her bedroom to finish getting ready. She pulled on a gray t-shirt that she selected from atop a colorful stack in the room's corner. Not bothering to dry her hair completely, it remained somewhat wet and dampened her shirt at the shoulders. She then stepped into a pair of denim overalls, choosing to fasten only one shoulder, before sliding on a pair of scuffed trainers, completing her minimalist ensemble. Then, taking a few long strides from the bedroom, she landed herself in the kitchen area. Her senses were first stricken by the smell of thick cut bacon, the sound of crackling resonating through the air as it cooked in a hot skillet, followed by a wave of smells coming from the accompaniments that Prue had prepared–eggs over easy, toasty hash browns, and French pressed coffee.

"Food'll be ready in a minute, dear. Have yourself a seat... or do whatever you wish! After all, today is *your* day," said Prue, singing nearly every word in her delight. Addy grinned. She knew Prue was excited for her birthday, but secretly knew that her grandmother was equally excited for bacon–one of her favorite foods.

Addy pulled a chair from the kitchen table. Before she could sit, she caught a glimpse of her neighbor and best friend, Eli, through the window of the front room, who was hurrying across the front of the house.

"Be right back, Gran," said Addy, prancing to the front door and flinging it open.

Addy stepped outside and was met with a gust of fresh air that brushed against her face. She spotted Eli the moment she opened the door, who was standing in the center of Addy's front lawn, hands planted on his hips. A fairly tall boy, albeit only slightly taller than Addy. He briefly shifted his gaze, revealing his gaunt face and flowing brown hair. His frame was firm, to say the least, as he was quite fit from a life of working on the farmstead that their families shared. His choice of attire was consistent–a pair of dark blue jeans

(Addy wasn't sure she'd ever seen him wear another pair), a white shirt, and a plaid button down. Today was no different, at least in that regard.

"Hey stranger," yelled Addy from the porch ironically, sauntering in his direction. "What brings you to this part of the yard?"

"Strangest thing out here is you," replied Eli, even more facetiously, if such a thing were possible. "Well, except, maybe, for this one here."

"Again? How many times is that now?"

"At least three that I can recall. I need to get him up before Magnus catches him out here again."

"And is Magnus awake?" asked Addy with a palpable sense of concern.

"No," said Eli curtly. "Drank himself to sleep last night. He shouldn't be up for a few more hours, but I'd rather be safe than sorry."

Eli bent his knees and hovered over the figure of a young boy–his brother, Luka–sleeping as soundly as one could on the wet grass of the front lawn. Eli gently grabbed his brother's shoulder, softly shaking him awake.

Luka's eyelids peeled back slowly. He squinted as he looked up at his brother, visibly annoyed at having been disturbed. Breaking eye contact, Luka looked about, and his eyes shot open with the recognition of not waking up in his bed, but rather outside the confines of his own home.

"Did–did it happen again?" asked Luka sweetly, trying to avert any sign of being in trouble.

"S' alright," reassured Eli, "I'm not sure how you can sleep out here though, nor am I sure how you manage to keep wandering off since the locks are all bolted shut. I wouldn't—"

"Next time, you might want to bring a pillow and a blanket," interrupted Addy, leaning over Eli's shoulder to see Luka.

"Addy!" shrieked Luka, springing to his feet and hugging her at the waistline. He was surprisingly alert and began talking quickly, ignoring the need to breathe.

"Happy Birthday! Did you get a lot of presents? Are you going to get a lot of presents? What are you doing today? Can we go into town later? Can we get ice cream? Can Mico come with us? Are you going to—"

"Clearly," said Eli, cutting Luka off before he could get another word in, "someone was so excited about your birthday, he came over to celebrate with you early, but didn't quite make it all the way." Eli ruffled Luka's bleach-blonde hair. Luka pushed his brother's hand away, flushed with embarrassment. "Our boy here did mention a few good ideas, though."

"As usual," said Addy, half-jokingly. Luka was even more brilliant than he was skilled at asking too many questions.

"You should let us take you to town for the day," said Eli. "It'll be fun. We'll poke around the tents, pop around the shops, go to the ice cream parlor..."

"Thanks," replied Addy, quick to cut Eli off, "but I have a lot of work to do today outback. You do remember what time of year it is, right?"

"Funny you should mention that..." said Eli innocently, scratching the back of his head. "Prue and I already took care of the fieldwork early this morning."

"It's true dear!" yelled Prue, who was now standing on the porch wielding a spatula. "You work hard enough as is, and, well, we wanted you to be free to enjoy your birthday. Who knows how many more of these we can all celebrate together?"

Addy knew her grandmother was being sincere, and that she and Eli were trying to make her feel special, but the comment had unintended consequences for Addy. Clever girl as she was, Addy had applied for a scholarship to an elite boarding school overseas, mostly to quell their persistent nagging. Both Eli and Prue had emphasized the importance of Addy realizing her dreams and recognized that her education was crucial for achieving them. Her grandmother and Eli were convinced she would get in, and truth be told, she wanted to attend more than she cared to admit. But more than that, Addy struggled with the concept of leaving them all behind, since she felt it would only be to *her* benefit.

"Breakfast is nearly finished. Best come in and eat before it gets cold," beckoned Prue. "There's plenty to go 'round, boys, if you fancy a bite."

"Thanks, Ms. Holt!" yelled Eli and Luka in unison as Prue scurried back into the house.

"I'd better go before she eats *all* the bacon," joked Addy. "You two coming?"

"Nah. Tell Prue thanks though," said Eli. "Got to put the feed out in the barn. Eat up and meet us out here in thirty?" Luka looked up at Addy with a gleaming sense of optimism. Her eyes rolled in amusement.

"I'll think about it. If I'm not out by then, you both know where I live."

Eli laughed, then nodded at Luka. Together, the boys scampered across the lawn and over a narrow dirt path separating the two farmstead homes. The houses sat less than a stone-throw away from one another, which Addy found rather odd considering the structures were the only ones for ages in any direction. Addy watched as the boys reached the house and tiptoed through the creaky front door, closing it gently behind them to ensure they would not stir their resting father.

As the door closed, Addy turned to face her own home and caught a glimpse of something rather strange. In the woods that lay across from the farmstead homes, sprawling front lawn, striated wood fence, and covered dirt road, she spotted two floating red orbs. Or at least that's what she believed at first, straining her eyes in observation, trying to figure out what else they could possibly be. As she blinked, the orbs vanished, leaving Addy to wonder if they had ever been there at all. *Were those red eyes that I saw?*

Pretending she hadn't noticed them to begin with, she looked away, snapping her gaze back, hoping to trick the objects into reappearing when she wasn't looking, but with no such luck. Mico began barking as Prue called Addy inside to eat. The prospect of disappointing Prue was more than enough for Addy to abandon any further investigation. She turned on her heel, marched to the front porch, walked past the old wooden door and, as she had done on more than one occasion that morning, put the thought that something strange was happening to her out of her mind.

Z.S. JOSEPH

3.

THE OGRE AND THE SPRITE

In a cavernous white lecture hall intended for the company of hundreds, only two men occupied the entire space. While a glance at their attire would lead one to believe that both men held a similar demeanor, both being outfitted in the same dark-navy tactical gear, their overall stature and underlying characteristics could not have been more opposite.

The first, a monstrous figure of a man by the name of Draven Burkhardt–or Burk, as he had come to be known–perched casually atop a marble desk at the front of the room. He held a glass tablet in one of his gorilla-sized hands, coolly swiping through virtual notes with the other.

Seeing Burk for the first time was nothing short of striking. Being alarmingly muscular and towering over most everyone whom he met was an afterthought compared to his most shocking feature. That title was held by the extensive scar that ran up the right side of his face. The gash unnervingly trailed over his right eye–the eye itself casting a ghostly shade of blue. Despite its prolonged presence, the wound looked fresh, deep, and horrifying. And while the scar was partially hidden by a thick, tidy beard, it did little to distract passersby from turning into gawkers, who found themselves perplexed as they pondered what could maim such a burly man. Gossip was plentiful amongst those who knew him least–an accident, no doubt, or perhaps an altercation with an equally large man wielding who knows what type of weapon. Many shuddered at the thought of there being two such formidable men in existence.

The second, far scrawnier man, went by the name of Sky Leto. Sky was the polar opposite of Burk–thin, arrogant, and foolhardy. He came from wealthy stock, which one could deduce from his meticulously groomed hair and his overall demeanor. Growing up, Sky's family shielded him from experiencing any of life's true hardships, often turning a blind eye to his imposing of hardship on others for his own alleged enjoyment. That same family had set aside a large sum of Valorem they had accrued over a millennium for an alleged singular purpose–a fund for philanthropic endeavors and charitable donations towards the betterment of mankind. The unspoken and more important truth of the matter is that those funds helped to secure the Leto family's elite status and maintain their power and influence. A large portion of that fund, no doubt, was directed to the Lookout Commission, which in turn had helped Sky in being accepted into the prestigious recruit program, which, as indicated on Sky's application, was a lifelong dream. And yet, Sky seemed none too eager to prove himself worthy of the role, as evidenced by his perfunctory level of effort–especially when it came to his studies–assuming himself a shoo-in and maintaining an elitist outlook towards work. He knew, regardless of applying more or less effort, that he was guaranteed to one day be in a comfortable position of power, whether that be a role with the Lookout Commission or elsewhere on high.

Sky's cavalier nature towards his training, driven by the weight of his family name, was a clear red flag for anyone in the Commission worth their salt to notice. Of those who knew the Leto family, either through personal experience or by name alone (those in the former group being few and far between), few were ambivalent to the family's nature or perceived intentions–the members of the Commission were no different in that regard. Those who despised them–and there were many–sought to distance themselves entirely. Those less fortunate souls who found themselves forced into dealings with the Leto family chose to keep their head down. However, those who were more ambitious, or perhaps desperate, seemed to associate themselves obsequiously with members of the Leto family, hoping their servitude would win them favor. An alliance that would without a doubt bring with it access to an abundance of resources and influences that could, in time, help those willing to pay the high price of admission.

Already a rarity in mind and appearance, Burk's position with the Leto family was one of limbo; a lone soldier, stationed between two disparate camps. Neither beguiled by excess, nor one to shy away from confrontation, Burk carried on in a conventional manner regardless of having a Leto family member in his presence. To Sky's chagrin, Burk unabashedly called upon the boy in the company of others as he would any recruit that crossed his path.

Perhaps that's the reason for our current predicament, Burk often thought. Much to his dismay, all senior officers of the Commission were responsible for training, at minimum, one recruit every five annos. While all senior officers were free to select whomever they wished from a pool of prospective candidates, Burk adamantly refused to waste his time with the selection process. As such, the Commission selected someone for him at random–a universal joke, and he was the bud of it.

Burk assumed that this time around, however, the process had not been random at all, but rather associated it with the inner workings of the Commission. Many of its esteemed members harbored negative thoughts about the Leto family, and only a few were unaware of Burk's unforgiving nature when it came to dealing with Sky. Thus, it would be reasonable to assume that someone had conducted their own silent revolt against the family by manufacturing the serendipitous relationship between the two–a role Burk had openly confessed was akin to being a glorified babysitter.

While Burk had frequently pawned Sky off on those in the lower ranks, allowing him to focus on matters he deemed more important, he was still not above the set of requirements that fell upon all other ranking members of the Commission: completing each recruit's core training, conducting a final assessment, and drawing up an evaluation report. All requirements that were on the brink of being overdue for Burk.

Sky sat in a desk chair a few paces from Burk. His chin rested on the palms of his hands while his right leg bounced up-and-down in boredom.

"This is boring...I'm bored," whined Sky.

"Then leave," said Burk dryly, who secretly hoped that Sky would seriously consider his advice. "You'll be kicked from the program and exiled from further engagements with the Commission. You'd be doing us both a favor." Burk didn't look up from his tablet, casually scrolling through its virtual pages as he spoke.

Sky shook off Burk's comment as if the desire for his departure hadn't been mentioned at all. Instead of confronting Burk head-on, Sky deduced pestering him would be far more interesting. Either that or he could continue sitting as though his time were of no importance. But why miss out on such a prime opportunity for fun?

In the time it took Burk to comb through another page, Sky had already Jolted, appearing behind the monstrous man in an instant as though he had teleported from his chair. He reappeared upright, standing closely behind Burk.

"Whatcha' looking at?" asked Sky, standing on his tiptoes to peer over Burk's bulging shoulder.

"Do that on Commission grounds again without my say

so," said Burk colorlessly, still not bothering to look up from his tablet, "and I promise you will be out of here faster than I can Jump to tomorrow, at which time, God willing, I'll be escorting you out of here personally."

"Word has it, that's pretty fast," said Sky curtly, testing Burk's patience. Intended result or not, Sky had pushed Burk against his tolerance threshold, which became clear as Burk looked up from his tablet and turned purposefully, meeting Sky's gaze with a deadly stare.

"Sit. Down."

Burk neither yelled nor raised his voice, but the manner of his response was more than enough to make the hair on the back of Sky's neck stand up. Eager to distance himself, Sky nearly Jolted back to his seat, but took a rare second to pause and think, wisely choosing to take the old-fashioned route. He moseyed back to his chair, took a seat, and crossed his arms like a toddler placed in a timeout.

"Now," said Burk calmly, looking back at his tablet. "Sky Leto. It probably comes as no surprise that your written and verbal test scores are, to put it bluntly, absolute shite."

"Well, I—" interrupted Sky, undoubtedly intending to make some sort of outlandish excuse. And while that approach may have worked countless times in his life, attempting to do so before Burk was nothing if not vain.

"It also did not go unnoticed by yours truly," continued Burk, his voice slightly elevating as he stood to his feet, "that many of the Commission's records highlighting your historical acts of impropriety were unintentionally *overlooked* by some of the higher-ups and have seemingly vanished. A recent, yet unsurprising development, and one I suppose we can chalk up to sheer luck.

"Or maybe it wasn't luck at all. The obvious alternative being rather clear, of course. You made it this far by falling under the protection and good-graces of some higher-power that recognized one of his little lambs had repented for a life of sin; and the almighty therefore decided, in all its infinite wisdom, to absolve you of your sins. Perhaps the family's contributions to the church didn't hurt your case, did it?"

"Watch yourself," Sky warned, "I might be a joke to you, but you can bet that any allegations against my family, *including me*, that my father will—"

"And finally!" roared Burk. "Lucky for me, the requirements ingrained in our program's feedback process are strictly confidential. Even the will of the almighty can't alter those. I've got a rather colorful picture of who you are, Sky. Your attitude and actions, both within and outside of my presence, have shown me the light. Seeing as you've probably had no real feedback in your entire privileged existence, I think it a worthy exercise to impart upon you some nuggets of truth."

Sky huffed and crossed his arms more tightly, looking towards the wall to show that Burk's words were of no importance.

"Let's see here...Ah, yes," continued Burk as he combed through his tablet. "Those with whom you partnered throughout the course of your training–recruits, mentors, and leadership alike–repeatedly noted a blatant disregard for standard protocols and a tendency to ignore direct orders. At one point or another, these unfortunate attributes almost caused the death of at least two other recruits. Lucky for you, or perhaps by the will of the almighty above, the official records of those circumstances seem to have changed in your favor. The blame passed on to others, despite your clear and inexcusable shortcomings."

Sky continued to sit and stare; he was trying to project confidence, to let Burk know his words meant nothing, and that the man was, by all accounts, beneath him in status. The attempt missed the mark, however, and Sky, unable to find the right words to form a valid response, appeared as nothing more than a pouting child. In the end, he fell back on what he did best, reverting to his old ways of threatening the opposition.

Finding a shred of confidence in himself, Sky replied, "Even you, Burk, legend or not, won't be able to keep me from—"

"Be that as it may," said Burk, toying with Sky and cutting him off from speaking yet again. "You also scored highest amongst the other Jolters in terms of raw abilities, which, I'll admit, isn't nothing." Burk carefully set his tablet down and casually made his way over to Sky. He grasped each side of the desk table, leaning intently to meet the young man directly at eye level.

"Now, we both know I'd rather you were finished with your training just as much as you would like me to sign-off on it. After that, as far as I'm concerned, you'll become someone else's problem." Burk whispered, yet his tone was deafening. "That said, I promise you this, *child*. If I catch wind of your antics, and those antics end up getting someone killed, true death or otherwise, I promise you, all the vals in the world won't be enough to keep me from carving your face up worse than what you see before you now."

Sky tried to remain calm, but couldn't stop himself from gulping reflexively. In a stroke of luck, the monitor on Burk's left forearm began to flash and emit an alarming sound, prompting Burk to step away from the desk, freeing Sky from his mentor's terrifying gaze.

Burk looked down at the blinking screen attached to his forearm. "That'll happen to you now and then–if you get your own compass, that is," said Burk, tapping on the screen and silencing the device. "That sound usually means you're running low on chrys…you'd know that by now if you opened a book once in a while. Stay here while I reload the module."

Burk strolled his way out of the lecture hall as Sky sat in silence, attempting to piece together his shattered ego.

Z.S. JOSEPH

4.
MEAT AND POTATOES

"Can I trouble you for the butter, dear?" asked Prue, reaching for a piece of toast, having already ravaged the bacon. Meanwhile Addy, having eaten far less than Prue, was unable to fathom how her petite grandmother could manage another bite, as she sat at the table, feeling full to the brim. Addy slowly inched her hand towards the silver tray of butter and slid it towards Prue.

"Gran," said Addy, "thank you for all of this. You really didn't have to go to all this trouble for me. I mean, don't get me wrong, I loved it, but with money being tight and all—"

"Hush now dear, you'll spoil your breakfast," asserted Prue as she buttered her toast. "And on that note, I must insist that you go into town with the boys to have yourself a spot of fun...And please don't worry about the money, dear, that's my job. Go and get yourself something nice for your birthday. If there's anyone at all that deserves it, my darling, it's certainly you." Prue winked at Addy, then took a bite of her butter-soaked toast.

"What about Mag–I mean, Mr. Smith?" asked Addy nervously. "He'll be a nightmare if he finds out that Eli used his truck to take us into town, today of all days. I know Eli can handle himself...but Luka. I don't want him to have to deal with any more of the man's nonsense than he does already. The way he acts this time of year is bad enough and, well, they shouldn't have to deal with any more of his craziness than they do already, especially not for me."

"That old fool? You let me worry about that, love," said Prue, "if any trouble comes about, Amico and I should be more than enough to keep Magnus from causing more of a ruckus than we can manage." At the mention of his full name, Mico, who had been sleeping next to the kitchen table, popped up at attention and rested his head on Addy's lap. She returned the action in kind, gently scratching him atop his head.

For a moment, they all sat together in silence–Addy petting Mico, Mico panting happily, and Prue alternating between munching her toast and sipping her tea. Everything was peaceful and everyone was content. The stillness of the moment gave Addy an opportunity to relax, which of course allowed her mind to wander, leading her to recall the underlying oddities of the morning–the dream about her parents, her eyes changing color overnight, her body overheating, Luka waking up in the front lawn. And did she actually see something glowing in the woods? Her mind couldn't seem to settle as she reflected on each distinct moment, some more thoroughly than others. Beginning to feel herself becoming anxious, she took a deep breath and let out an inaudible sigh.

Addy's thoughts were interrupted as the front door squeaked open.

"Ready then, Ads?" asked Eli, leaning to cross the threshold of the house from the front porch without actually stepping foot inside. "Luka's in the truck waiting."

"Best be off then, dear," said Prue, standing to embrace her. "Have a lovely time my darling," she continued, hugging Addy tightly and looking over her shoulder at Eli. "You will take care of our sweet Adelynne here, Eli. Yes?"

"Of course, Ms. Holt," said Eli, "I'll be sure to get the kids home safe." Addy rolled her eyes in playful irritation.

"Thank you, Eli," said Prue, offering a smile and nod of approval. "Happy Birthday, my dear," she continued to Addy, releasing her embrace before taking Addy by the hand. "I know you didn't know them, darling, but your parents would have been so proud of you." Addy blushed and hugged Prue once more, thanked her for breakfast, then left with Eli to meet Luka in the truck.

Prue stood on the front porch, waving Addy, Eli, and Luka off as they puttered down the road in the cab of a rusty pickup. No sooner after the truck's rear lights faded in the distance, Prue's ears were met with a startling bang. She looked across the yard and saw the front door of the opposing home shoot open like a cannon. Magnus, roused by the sound of the old truck's backfiring exhaust, stumbled onto the porch as inelegantly as one could manage, then plopped down into a nearby rocking chair.

Magnus leaned over in his seat, elbows on knees and hands on chin, and stared out at the road. He fidgeted for a bit, slicked back his greasy, peppered hair, then grabbed a flattened pack of cigarettes from his pocket. Packing the box against his wrist, Magnus scanned across the front lawns of the homestead and spotted Prue idling on her front porch.

"Alright then, Prudence," said Magnus, lighting his cigarette. "Happen to know where my truck is?"

"Good morning, Magnus," replied Prue calmly, strolling over to meet him. "Hungover today, are we? I'm sure you'll recall our having a conversation about the truck–though I wouldn't expect you to these days. Perhaps Addy's birthday, of all things, may ring a bell?"

"Hmph," breathed Magnus in annoyance, flicking ash from his cigarette.

"You haven't drunken yourself into enough of a state to have forgotten the date already?" asked Prue. "Honestly Magnus, of all the days—"

"OF COURSE," yelled Magus, "of course. Yes, I know what day it is, Prudence. For once, can you just leave it? Just once? At least give me that, woman."

"Magnus..." said Prue gently, placing her hand on his shoulder. "It's been what, 'round a decade or so that we've had these little tiffs? You know I will always be here for you, dear, but to go it alone like this every year? It's not my place, but it's rather confusing to the boys and Addy alike. How're they supposed to understand? Addy, thinking she's somehow to blame. And your boys, not knowing what happened to their mother. Honestly, Magnus, not telling your children—"

"*My children?*" laughed Magnus mirthlessly.

"Don't," warned Prue, waving her finger at Magnus. "Magnus. Don't you dare! You and Ira raised those boys. Raised them in a good and loving home. To grow up and be decent. She thought the world of you–all of us did, the boys included, though they don't remember. What would she think, Magnus, to see you now?"

"Are you going to tell me where my truck is or not?" asked Magnus, taking a long draw from his cigarette, letting smoke and silence fill the space between them.

"Very well, Magnus," said Prue somberly. "Yes, the boys have the truck. They're taking Adelynne into town for her birthday. If you won't be telling them what happened and if you're set on drinking yourself into a stupor, then I insist you give them the courtesy of being able to enjoy the day without worrying about you getting your knickers in a twist. And I swear, Magnus, if you get out of line with those boys again, there will be hell to pay."

Prue started her way back towards her house, pausing halfway.

"I'm taking Amico with me out to the fields to pick fresh

strawberries for Adelynne's cake," said Prue, looking over her shoulder. "I'll also be stopping by to pay Ira a visit. It's a perfect day to bring her some fresh flowers. I'm sure she'd like it if you joined me."

Having heard enough, Magnus finished his cigarette, flicked the butt towards the lawn, and turned back to enter the house without a word.

"Stubborn old fool," whispered Prue. She shuffled across the dirt driveway and climbed the short set of stairs to her porch. As she took hold of the front door handle, she heard a dull rustling from behind and looked back in suspense, hoping with all her heart to find that Magnus had changed his mind.

"Mustn't yet get our hopes up," she mumbled under her breath. She looked over her shoulder in disappointment for a moment, then strode back inside her house.

5.

THE GREMLIN

"Hello, Janice. Nice to see you," said Burk halfheartedly, cracking a false smile. "I seem to be out of Chrysalix at the moment. Can I bother you for a refill? The usual should do, love, then I'll be on my way."

Burk spoke to a small, grimy old woman sitting behind an oversized marble counter opposite where he stood. He could barely make out Janice's face from behind the sea of computer screens scattered about her workspace, as his view was impeded by a dense, lingering smog resultant of the woman's incessant smoking habit. Past Janice's desk, beyond the smoke, Burk could see a towering, silvery wall, decorated with a freshly painted emblem resembling an eye centered around a ticking clock. The same emblem adorned each side of Burk's shoulder armor as the primary symbol of the Lookout Commission. Burk squinted at the wall, then back down to the desk. Waiting for Janice to respond, he inspected the top of the desk to keep busy, taking his time to look over a tiny wooden sign with golden-clad font that read: *JANICE MOKES, HEAD ADMINISTRATIVE OVERSEER.*

Janice hardly registered that someone was speaking to her, acknowledging the request only after recognizing the towering man before her. She clamped down on a lever underneath her hover chair, her cigarette dangling between her lips, nearly flying away as she rocketed upwards.

"Commanda Burk," groaned Janice, "always wantin' somethin', just like da rest of 'em." She flashed her crooked teeth playfully at Burk. "Yea', I can help ya'. Gimme a minute to pull up ya' file."

Janice pulled the lever on her chair, plummeting until she hovered at eye level with the screen that she was previously mesmerized by. She turned around to find an idle computer monitor and splayed her hands and fingers outward towards the black screen–the motion prompting a holographic keyboard to appear before her. She took a deep draw from her cigarette as she typed. Burk's face popped up on the once lifeless screen. A windmill of files and circuit-like paths flew about beside his image, arranging themselves in an orderly manner on the leftmost side of the screen.

"Alrighty, Burky boy," said Janice as she continued to type and talk through puffs of livid smoke, "looks like I can give ya' what you want...but I think we both know what I need from ya' first."

"Haven't a clue, Janice," he replied playfully. "We both know I'm not as well suited on such matters as you. Why don't you tell me what it is you need, exactly?" Of course, Burk had an inkling what she was referring to, but he would not risk bringing up some other matter he was already delinquent on.

Janice stopped typing. Turning to face Burk, she took a long puff and shot upward. She leaned on the countertop and held her breath, exhaling smoke in his direction. "Don't be all coy wit' me," she garbled, flicking ash in whatever direction seemed to suit her. "Ya' may look like half an oga', but we both know ya' smarter than one. Gimme ya' report on the Leto boy and I'll set ya' up with some of 'at sweet lyx."

"It'll be a few more days before that's all sorted, love," said Burk calmly. Janice paused, turning her attention from the monitor towards Burk.

"Burk," said Janice slowly, taking on a much more serious tone. "I don't think I need ta' tell ya' how important it is for you to get the Leto kid troo 'da 'cruit program."

Despite Burk's status as a high-ranking member of the Lookout Commission, even he was at the mercy of Janice. Her primary role as head admin was dedicated to making sure that *everyone* followed protocol. She had devoted more than half a century establishing a title and name for herself in that department and, despite her gremlin-like demeanor, she wasn't about to tarnish her name and reputation by breaking the rules, especially if the Leto family was involved. And while that may have been an open and shut case for anyone else, Burk knew he could win the woman over and bend the rules in his favor if he played nice.

Janice leaned in, beckoning Burk to join her. Burk leaned

in to meet Janice–the aroma of her breath caused his eyes to water. "Even I got my orders ta' make sure ya' boy gets troo," she whispered cautiously, pointing towards the ceiling, her cigarette drooping between her fingers. "I've been 'ere too damn long ta' question 'em–and 'tween us gals' I think ya' know who's makin' sure we got the vals to keep the wheels turnin' in this place. Don't know about you, but I ain't about ta' be the one to bite the hand."

Janice leaned away from Burk and ashed her cigarette on the floor.

"Get it done," she demanded. "Ya' do dat, and I'll get ya' on ya' way to bigga' and betta' things, just how ya' like it," she smirked.

"That's all well and good, love," said Burk, "but we both know I'm going to need a refill before then to finish the boy's training. Tell me how we can help each other in the meantime, love, and I'll be on my way. I'm sure there's something I can do to make life easier for the both of us."

Before Burk had finished his sentence, Janice turned and glided towards a screen on her right, thrusting her hands outward to type on a projected keyboard. "Tell ya' what," she said, "I gots plenty of D&M's that need ta' be looked inta'. Ya' gotta take ya' 'cruit with ya' on at least one assignment–even orders from on high can't change that. In your case, it looks like ya' 'cruit needs a refresha' in protocol before graduatin' from the program. For everyone's sake, go check things out at a couple spots. I'll give ya' lyx *and* I'll be plenty lenient on ya' report."

"And *when* exactly would I be taking him?" asked Burk, more impatiently than he was going for.

"Has to be the Past," replied Janice. "Got plenty of Pre-Col' ripples built up and finding anyone–er–assigning folks ta' task hasn't gotten any easier."

Burk steadied himself, holding his breath to stifle his groan. Detect and Monitor missions were one thing, but doing it in the Past was a different story. Traveling into Pre-Collision territory required too many Pushes and Jumps, wasted precious time and resources, and whatever they were going to investigate almost always turned out to be some less-than-noteworthy cosmic anomaly that wasn't worth the effort. As far as he was concerned–and many others for that matter–anything or anyone in the Past that was worth looking into had already been dealt with.

Then Burk had an epiphany. If he *had* to take Sky with him on assignment, what could be better than a bit of quiet D&M? Doing nothing isn't an option, he realized, but going on assignment to a time and place where they didn't need to do much of anything other than sit and observe would ensure he could keep Sky close under his watch. And even if Sky did something sporadic and uncalled for, it would have little to no impact on the Timeline, keeping himself off the radar from those on high while bringing him another step closer to closing the books on his direct involvement with Sky–and with any luck, the Leto family entirely.

"Actually, Janice," grinned Burk, "that sounds lovely."

Z.S. JOSEPH

6.

GROWING PAINS

"Where is it we're going again, exactly?" asked Sky, struggling to keep pace with Burk as they strutted down one of the many narrow and brightly lit halls of the Commission.

"*When*, Sky...always when. Worry about the 'where' when we get there," said Burk, "but since you asked so nicely... the Past. Somewhere around two-hundred years Before Collision as far as I can tell. We'll know more once we get to the prep zone."

"Where–I mean–er–*when* is two-hundred years Before Collision?" asked Sky hesitantly, regretting his decision at the sight of Burk rolling his eyes.

"Christ of old," said Burk, "how is it you got accepted into the Commission? Better yet...don't answer that. Two-hundred B.C., Sky, is approximately 138 annos before the Collision. You do know what the Collision is, yes? Or do I have to explain that to you as well?"

"C'mon, Burk. Even I know the basics," said Sky. A look of skepticism dawned on Burk's face. "The Collision almost wiped humanity out of existence," continued Sky, "although it did come with the added benefit of new abilities, which I'm rather fond of all things considered." Burk raised his brow in response, causing Sky to fall back a few paces out of Burk's view to avoid the possibility of any follow-up questions.

After marching down hallway after hallway, Burk finally stopped in front of a bulky metal door. Next to its frame, a holographic keypad projected from the wall–a camera lens sat in place directly above it. Burk punched a code into the keypad with his index finger and the keypad flashed bright red. He entered another code...then another...and then another...

"Hate these bloody things," murmured Burk to himself.

"Everything alright there, sir?" asked Sky flippantly.

Burk ignored him, focusing his attention on bypassing the door. He lifted his left forearm, bringing his monitor at eye level, and began typing, prompting a long string of code to appear. He pinched his monitor, enlarging the coded image until it projected into the air, then placed the projection in front of the camera lens.

Seconds later, the door hissed as steam rolled around its edges. The metal frame fell back a smidge and crept open. Cold air slammed the two men in the face as icy fog wafted its way out of the room. Before the door opened fully, Burk walked confidently into the pitch-black chamber on the other side. Sky hesitantly followed, keeping close to Burk as they crossed the doorframe's icy threshold.

As they entered the room, the door moved back in the other direction, vacuum sealing shut behind them. Lights that were scattered across the ceiling blinked repeatedly, struggling to stay aflame in the frosty atmosphere. Before long, they stabilized, finally revealing the room's contents. Each wall was completely flat and made of poured concrete, making the room feel chillier and less inviting with each passing moment.

Opposite the door they had entered, much of the wall was filled from floor to ceiling with monitors of varying design, all with an underlying similarity to the one attached to Burk's arm. As intriguing as that was, the center of the room was the main attraction. Among the sea of gray sat a menacing contraption–a leather-fitted medical recliner surrounded by robotic arms and metal claws. Aside from it sat a shiny, hovering cart topped with neatly organized surgical tools. Beyond the medieval setup stood a tiny platform, fitted atop a bulky, standalone computer terminal.

"Take a seat," ordered Burk, motioning towards the center of the room. Sky surveyed his surroundings, praying for an undiscovered seat, before cautiously approaching the menacing chair. He took a deep breath before sliding into place, squirming and shivering as the room grew colder.

"I'm sure you've put together by now that this room is

where we keep the S.T. Configuration Modules," said Burk, grabbing one of the units off of the wall and bringing it back to the station at the center of the room. "That's the technical name, anyway. Most everyone in the field refers to them as either a module or compass."

"Am-m-m–I–g-g–getting a c-c-compass?" chattered Sky, the room feeling more and more like a glorified refrigerator intended to store him as frozen meat.

"You are indeed," said Burk, pausing at the computer station to hit a few buttons with his free hand. "There are a multitude of uses for these devices. I'm sure you'll be able to recall all of them–they are, in fact, part of the basics you seem to be so well read on."

Burk moved towards the chair and set the lengthy module down on the silver table, then circled back around to the standalone computer. "As a refresher course, you'll only need to know a few things. First, the unit will help you understand when you are on the Timeline. If that location has been surveyed, then most of the devices can also tell you where you are on the planet with near pinpoint geographical accuracy. Now put your arms out flat and sit still."

Sky complied with Burk's command and laid his arms flat on either side of the chair's armrests. Moments passed where all he could hear was Burk pounding away at the keyboard. In an instant, thick metal straps shot outward from the chair, securing Sky's body to it. Sky's eyes widened in panic as the sound of the metal arm beside him roared to life, floating across him to grasp the tabled module with its massive claws.

"Second," continued Burk, speaking more loudly to overcome the whirs of the instruments, "you'll come to find that using your abilities in the Past isn't easy without chrys, and can often be near impossible, even for the best of us. The unit is fitted with a repository to store chrys, which is then harnessed and redistributed internally, allowing you to use your abilities freely. Mind, in your case, each time you Jolt you'll drain a portion of chrys, which you won't be able to recharge in the Past due to the Earth's climate, so you'll need to do so sparingly when the time comes. Best that you keep an eye on your resource levels until you get a feel for how much the unit can handle."

Sky paid minimal attention to Burk, mesmerized by the mechanical menace hovering above him. The claws separated the compass in half on the table; the edge of each component laden with jutting and jagged pieces that had once interconnected as though two pieces of an intricate puzzle. The claw widened from its center, lowering each piece of the monitor into position on either side of Sky's left forearm. It hissed as it slowed to a halt and rested in place. Two thick, pronged spikes revealed themselves from the underside of each distinct piece.

"And, finally," said Burk, pausing to look up from the computer terminal. "This is going to hurt."

Burk pushed a button with his index finger. Steam shot from the sides of the robotic assistant. The metal arms screamed as each side of the claw slammed towards one another, rejoining the device around Sky's fleshy forearm.

"*AAAAAAARRRGGGHHHHHH!*"

Sky squealed in agony, struggling to escape the confinement of his seat. A whirring screech stirred from under the device as the two-pronged pieces drilled their way into Sky's arm, ceasing only after they had penetrated his bones. The twisting stopped, giving way to the faint sound of cracking as the spikes settled in the marrow. Burk hardly paid attention as Sky looked at him in agony. Sky tried to writhe free from the horrific sensation, imagining his pain being akin to the final nails being driven into a coffin. His mouth fell open, and he attempted to scream, but what manifested instead were intermittent squeaks and gasps of ice cold air.

Burk casually typed away at the keyboard before forcefully pressing another large button. Sky's head shot back, lifting his chest off the chair towards the ceiling. Burk knew the boy would get the worst of it at this stage. An immense heat would build inside the recruit's body, which, at its breaking point, would disperse and expand from the device's entry point, surging throughout the entirety of his internal ecosystem.

Sky cried out again at the unbearable feeling of being burned from the inside out, feeling at any moment he may be subject to combustion. He cried out again at the sight of the metal claw's wild movements, pleading with Burk to take the unit off. The claws began welding the device together; Sky's eyes rolling into the back of his head.

"Stay awake a few more seconds there, chap," said Burk loudly to Sky over the sound of the clanking robot.

Just as Sky neared unconsciousness, the heat inside him subsided. A pleasant cooling sensation took over, creating a sense of euphoria, calming him back to consciousness and into the comfort of his seat. The metal claws emitted a menthol scented gel, clearing away any pain that had once radiated from under the device. Finally releasing Sky's forearm from their grip, the claws loosened. Sky slouched in his chair, gasping for breath, before eventually losing consciousness.

"Handled that about as well as anyone," said Burk.

Z.S. JOSEPH

7.
EBB AND FLOW

"We're almost there," said Eli, lightly nudging Luka on the shoulder with one hand while the other maintained a firm grip on the steering wheel.

"I'm just glad we made it in one piece in this thing," said Addy, sincerely happy to be near their destination after spending nearly an hour in the shaky truck.

"What? This old bird?" said Eli, "listen, if she can survive the abuse she's gotten from Magnus' driving, she can survive just about anything."

Addy gazed out of the passenger window and cranked the knob on the door. The window jerked as it rolled down, eventually disappearing behind the door frame, freeing Addy to stick her arm through the opening. She let her hand ride the waves of the cool summer breeze, rested her arm alongside the passenger door, and closed her eyes. Poking her head out to feel the calm air blow on her face and through her hair, she forgot altogether of her desire to escape the confines of the wobbly truck.

SKKKKKKKKKRRRRRRTTTTTTT

The tail of the truck skidded violently. Addy's eyes flew open as she yanked herself against the force of gravity back into the car. Luka shot up from his slumber, flailing in confusion. Eli skillfully turned the steering wheel back and forth to gain control, avoiding a dangerously large tree branch obstructing their path.

"Woah," exclaimed Eli, bringing the car back under his control, "what the hell was that?!"

"A tree branch, Eli!" squawked Addy, looking in the rear window back at the debris in the road. "Clearly, I spoke too soon about arriving in one piece."

"Sorry, sorry," said Eli, "I swear there was nothing there a minute ago. It's like that branch just—never mind. Must've dozed off...getting sleepy from the drive I 'spose. We'll be there soon."

Add one more thing to the growing list of odd things that've happened today, thought Addy.

A few more minutes of delicate travel passed before the group turned off the main road and pulled into a half empty parking lot. Eli quickly found an empty space and parked the truck. Addy and Luka wasted no time dashing out of the vehicle as soon as Eli had shifted into park, both relieved to be back on solid, unmoving ground.

The town they had arrived at was neither big nor bustling. However, for Addy, Eli, and Luka, who spent most of their days on their secluded farmstead, the town had become a sight to behold. An avenue ran its way through the center of the town, with a clay sculpted water fountain stationed at the midpoint, littered with jumping dolphins and soaring birds, each spouting water in a high arc back down into the main basin. One side of the avenue was lined with a strip of colorful shops and restaurants–on the other side, a row of canvas tents whose entrances flapped about in the wind, each brandished with colorful signage flashing the type of wares they traded in.

"Where we headed then?" asked Eli.

"Can we go get ice cream?" asked Luka with an angelic tone.

"It's a bit early for that, my wee man, but we can get some later. It's Addy's birthday, so let her have the first pick, eh?" said Eli, giving his brother a wink. "After you, madam," he continued to Addy, motioning with his arm in an overly chivalrous manner.

"Why thank you, sir. This way then," said Addy, making an exaggerated gesture for Eli and Luka to follow her towards the row of tents.

Luka tugged on the sleeve of Eli's shirt to get his attention. Eli, knowing full well what his younger brother wanted, hoisted the young boy up onto his shoulders.

"Oof, you've grown quite a bit," said Eli, "not sure how

much longer I can keep doing this." The brothers chuckled, then Eli marched forward with his brother perched securely on his shoulders, taking long strides to catch up with Addy.

As the tents drew near, Addy's attention shifted towards the nearest entrance where a woman could be seen restraining a small boy by the arm. The boy was wailing and pointing up at a rather tall, bearded man wearing sunglasses and a flat cap. Ignoring the woman and child, the man remained motionless with his hands stiff inside his coat pockets, keeping his eyes forward. The woman wrestled the child into her arms before making her way towards the man, shaking a stern finger at him.

A hefty gust of wind curved its way around the bend in the road, blowing past the tents and towards Addy. The tent's opening flaps stirred and thrashed, briefly obstructing Addy's view of the unfolding commotion before her. Addy, feeling rather nosy but more so intrigued by the matter, remained fixated on their location.

As the wind died down, the flapping faces of the tents came to a standstill, revealing an empty space where the man, woman, and child had once occupied.

"Um," started Addy, "Eli, did–did you see the three people up there just now?"

"What people?" asked Eli, making his way up to her side. "Plenty of folks are around, Ads. You'll have to be more specific."

"It was like a magic trick," replied Addy in bewilderment.

"There was a man, and a woman with a little kid standing in front of that tent. You didn't see them?"

"Didn't see a thing, no," replied Eli. "You said they were at the entrance? 'Spose they went inside then."

"Sure, no, you're probably right," agreed Addy reluctantly, unsure whether or not she should inquire further at the risk of sounding like a lunatic. *I'm clearly looking for things that aren't there*, she thought, recalling the strange occurrences from the morning.

"We can go check if you want to," said Eli, sensing her hesitation. "They ought to have some interesting knick-knacks in there. Worth browsing the tents from front to back, anyway."

Addy made her way into the tent, followed by Eli, who had to stoop so he and his brother could make their way through the entrance. Inside, the tent was organized into wide rows spaced between wooden trestle tables, overflowing with cardboard boxes of various shapes and sizes. Each box held a random assortment of throwaway items worth as much as anyone would pay for them.

At the back of the shop, the tent the flaps had parted, creating an opening for the light to shine through and space for patrons to exit. To the far right, a shopkeeper stood behind a wooden counter, staring at the entrance to cast judgment upon all who entered his domain.

"Oi," shouted the shopkeeper, "You! No mucking about in 'ere. Put 'at boy down or find yourselves elsewhere."

"Sorry!" replied Eli, helping his brother off his shoulders.

"No one but us in here," remarked Addy to Eli, ignoring the shopkeeper. "I don't see those people anywhere, do you?" she asked rhetorically.

"There's an exit...see?" remarked Eli, motioning towards the back of the shop. "They must've popped in and out."

"Oh, look at this!" said Luka. He lunged towards a table, pulled the nearest box to his chest, and rummaged through the contents to reveal a toy laser, brandishing it with a triumphant grin. He pointed it up at Eli and Addy, taking aim and squeezing the trigger, causing the toy to glow and emit high-pitched tings and zaps. Addy, having forgotten the reason they had entered the tent in the first place, grabbed another laser from the box and began firing back at Luka. Eli surrendered to them both, raising his hands high in the air.

"Oi! What'd I tell you lot?" the shopkeeper yelled at them from afar. "Shut your box of toys! You touch something, you best be showing me some bees and honey!"

The three of them chuckled and placed the toys back in the box. Having had enough of the shopkeeper's oversight, they thanked him for letting them have a look around, then left in search of another tent.

For the next few hours, the trio browsed the rest of pop-ups, each shopkeeper far more welcoming than the first they had met–and with much more lax policies. While each canvas storefront had the same layout, a row of tables topped with a multitude of various crates and cardboard boxes, the contents of each were unique. The second tent they entered, where Luka and Addy held a miniature fashion show, contained flamboyant scarves and hats. The next, sports equipment, which prompted a game of floor hockey with the shopkeeper keeping goal. Later, comics and video games from every era imaginable, along with a free-to-play retro arcade machine, powered by a rather noisy generator, equipped with an assortment of vintage games–all of which Luka bested them at.

Having cruised through every tent, they exited the last in the row and made their way towards the shops across the street. Dark clouds swirled overhead, blocking out the earlier abundance of sunshine. The once barren road was now congested with traffic, and the three crossed the street to the center avenue, waiting patiently for cars to pass.

Addy felt a single drop of rain on her cheek, followed by a light drizzle, which eventually crescendoed into a torrential downpour. Staying alert to the traffic in the street, she rushed to find an opening to cross the road and seek refuge. Straining to look past the rain, she caught a glimpse of something by the avenue's central fountain. Resting upon it, hands firmly in his pockets, was the tall, bearded man that she assumed had vanished earlier in the day. While the day's events had put her intrigue aside, her curiosity was once again piqued as the man sat and stared onward, looking beyond the heavy rain in her direction.

Addy, entranced in thought, jumped aside in surprise as two drivers stopped in the street, bringing the flow of oncoming traffic to an abrupt stop. The driver honked his car horn, lurched over the car's steering wheel, and motioned forward for the group to cross.

"Let's go!" yelled Eli, grabbing Addy by the arm, pulling her and Luka onto the street.

Addy dashed across the slick pavement and onto the safety of the sidewalk, then spun on her heel to look back towards the fountain and find the tall, bearded man once more. Her eyes met a group of gaggling teenagers running to safety, passing the fountain's front and obstructing her view before clearing away to reveal an empty space where the man once sat.

"Addy, come on!" yelled Eli, holding the door of the nearest shop open for her to enter. She snapped out of her trance, spun around, and made her way through the door to join Eli and Luka, the three of them shivering, cold, and wet at the shop's entrance.

"Ahem!"

A voice squeaked from behind the turquoise counter near the entrance of the shop. Turning, the group spotted the source of the noise as a portly woman in a red feathered dress. Her nostrils flared as she glared at them with disdain, her beady eyes bearing down on them through her cat eye shaped spectacles.

"This shop is for patrons only!" sang the woman. "What is it you're doing here?"

"Sorry, ma'am," said Eli, shivering from the combination

of wet clothes and cold air blasting from a nearby air-conditioner. "It just started to rain, ma'am...would you mind letting us stay here for a minute until it passes?"

The paunchy woman, standing on an elevated platform behind the counter, inspected them one-by-one to cast her judgment. After looking at a shivering, doe eyed Luka, she eased the contortions of her face and forced a crooked smile.

"Fine," hissed the woman, "once the rain stops and not a minute more! Do take care to stay *exactly* where you are–and don't touch anything unless you intend to buy it." She stormed off to the back room, leaving the three of them standing at the entrance, dripping water all over the shop floor.

"Eli," whispered Addy, "did you happen to see that man at the fountain?"

"No, I was a bit concerned with trying to stay dry, thank you," said Eli. "What man was it?"

"I think it was the same guy I saw earlier," replied Addy, "I don't know–it seemed like he was looking at me. I didn't notice last time, but he was standing and staring in the rain and he didn't seem to be concerned at all about getting drenched."

"Hmmm," pondered Eli, taking a moment to respond. "You do seem a little spooked."

"We'll protect you, Addy!" said Luka.

"Oh, you will, will you?" said Addy playfully.

"Tell you what," said Eli, "I'll keep an eye out, yeah? If I see this man of yours anywhere, I'll be sure to let you know. Promise."

After the heavy downpour turned into a light drizzle, the woman returned to shoo the group out of the shop, voicing her displeasure at the pool of water they had left behind for her to clean up. Bit by bit, the rain ceased entirely, with the clouds dissipating to reveal warming rays of sunshine. The wind subsided, and the lack of breeze made way for humidity to set in the air.

"I'd say it's about time for that ice cream," said Addy to Luka, patting him on the head and giving him a nod. Luka smiled and darted down the street, making his way towards the front of a building branded with a large mural of a rainbow flowing into a vanilla ice-cream cone. Using all his might, Luka struggled with the weight of the building's front door. He yanked it open with the help of a patron exiting the building before making a gleeful sprint inside.

"He's been waiting all day for you to say that," said Eli, strolling casually alongside Addy as they made their way down the street.

"I'm surprised he made it this long," joked Addy before instinctually looking about in search of the tall, bearded man.

"I don't see him, Ads," said Eli, taking notice of her being distracted. "The man you're looking for, I mean."

"Oh–thanks," replied Addy, "I don't see him either."

Taking their time to dry off, the two meandered past the pastel-colored shops. When they made it to the ice cream parlor, the most vibrant building in the row, Eli held the door open for Addy, following her through the entrance.

Addy and Eli had just made it past the doorway when they first caught sight of him. There, at the front of the line, leaning with one arm on the glass counter, was the tall, bearded man in a flat cap.

Z.S. JOSEPH

8.
A HOUSE OF HOUDINI

"I swear, if you pull some shit like that on me again without warning," started Sky to Burk as they made their way to another room. Sky's former sense of euphoria, caused by the drugs the device had pumped into him earlier, had worn off, making him quite irritable as the pains of being grafted to his newfound technological sidekick rebounded. "I swear, Burk, I swear I'll—"

"What?...What'll you do, Sky?" said Burk with an undertone of disgust. "You'll do nothing, that's what. Don't forget your place, boy. I've just given you a gift and you're complaining? And what about...A bit of pain? Try it. Threaten me again and I promise. You do that, and I'll show pain beyond your imagination. You'll wish you were back in that chair by the time I've only just started with you."

"We'll see about that, old man," pouted Sky quietly under his breath, careful to make sure Burk didn't hear him.

The two turned a corner, and Burk came to a halt. He threw a large, clenched fist in the air, signaling the command for Sky to stop behind him. Burk took two steps forward and entered a code into a keypad beside a far less burly door than the one that had protected the room they'd visited earlier. This time, after one attempt, the keypad flashed green, and the door clicked open, prompting the two men to enter.

Burk and Sky walked through a short hallway before finding themselves in the middle of a vast, circular room. Sky looked around in awe at the sight before him. The surrounding white-washed walls had been carved from the inside out of the massive wooden tree they now found themselves in, creating rows of rectangles with vivacious designs, each appearing distinct from one another at first glance. As Sky looked upward, the rectangular formation revealed a twisting circular design that extended as far as the naked eye could see. At the top, light beamed through, casting itself down between a sea of vibrant red leaves.

Sky craned his head back and looked up at the ceiling in awe, unable to make out anything but shadow as the rectangular wooden lockers faded into darkness.

"How do all these rectangles make a circle?" asked Sky.

Burk groaned and started towards the center of the room where another terminal stood. Sky leaned beside it while Burk placed the display of his compass against the terminal glass. A moment later, two distinct pops sounded from above, echoing throughout the chamber.

Burk looked down at the terminal where a message flashed on the screen: *2036A AND 2036B.* He tapped on the terminal, causing Sky to jerk forward and almost lose his balance. Burk and Sky stood in the confines of a stationary circle at the center of the room as the outer edge of the floor began rotating. The once stationary floor hissed and hovered in place. Burk tapped the screen once more, and the floor spun before ascending at a rapid pace, quickening with each rotation and hurdling the men up towards the heavens.

Once a vivid and mesmerizing scene, the walls of the room blurred, becoming unrecognizable with each passing moment. The speed of the rotating floor and upward acceleration picked up so much that the surrounding designs blended together into a dense wall of black. Sky put his hands outward to keep himself from falling, feeling with his fingers to cling to a piece of the terminal for support. Burk, unfazed, stood still–his only movement being that of a raised eyebrow as he stared at the struggling recruit in amusement.

Almost as soon as it had started, the floor came to a grinding halt. Sky, close to losing his balance again, tried to seem unimpressed as he looked back at Burk, who stood coolly in the center of the room.

"Follow me," said Burk, walking past Sky towards the lockers behind them. "You take 2036B." Burk pushed against a rectangle with the numbers 2036A carved across its header. The rectangular door set back before swinging open. Sky watched Burk carefully and followed suit. Each wooden locker contained a folded pile of clothes, purple microchip, collapsible nightstick, silver ration packets, black circular sunglasses, leather wallet, metallic canteen, shoulder bag, and a manila envelope with the crest of the Commission stamped on the cover. Burk removed the contents from the cupboard and turned back to the center of the room. A slab of tile floated to Burk's right, where he placed the assortment of acquired items.

Sky grabbed the contents from his own locker and closed it shut. He turned to see that Burk had placed his items on a table, then searched around to find his own. He was surprised to see the table descending and stared in confusion as it dropped and reintegrated with the rest of the marble floor.

"Shit," muttered Sky, irritated that Burk had not warned him about keeping the locker door open. Burk rolled his eyes and made room on his marble table, motioning at an open spot for Sky to place his things.

"So...are you gonna tell me what we're doing, exactly?" asked Sky, setting down the contents of his locker.

Burk grunted, signaling to Sky that this was information he should have known already. "Well, young Sky," said Burk as he removed his clothes, "this is one of the many Lookout Commission prep zones. That is what we're doing–preparing."

"Why do we have to change clothes?" asked Sky, holding up a pair of blue jeans in wonder.

"We've been tasked with a D&M run," replied Burk,

unbuttoning his shirt. "It's fairly straightforward–there are only two steps. I imagine even you will be able to keep track of that much, yes?"

Sky looked past his jeans to glare at Burk.

"First," continued Burk, "we go to the source of any detected ripples, survey the scene, and identify what's caused them."

"Ripple?" questioned Sky.

"Christ, boy," sighed Burk. "A ripple, Sky, is caused by an inordinate amount of energy that creates detectable anomalies in spacetime. Those anomalies, depending on their size and nature, have the potential to impact the Timeline. Do try to keep up as I explain step two."

Sky ignored Burk's sharp remarks and inspected his new garments.

"If we determine the cause of the ripple to be a natural occurrence, we document it and take our leave. If not, that means someone is likely the cause of it, and we handle the situation in a manner deemed to be most appropriate." In his heyday, Burk had suggested there should be another letter at the end of D&M to illustrate how these types of missions can unfold. *May as well tag on an 'E' for engage*, he thought, having deemed it an appropriate addition to the acronym. Nowadays, he had little interest in spending his time arguing semantics with the likes of someone like Janice to change it.

"Handle the–what do you mean?" asked Sky excitedly, struggling to pull on a pair of tightly fitted blue jeans.

"Those are on backwards," said Burk, causing Sky to redden with embarrassment. "What do you think I mean by *situation*, if you had to fancy a guess?"

Sky stopped in his tracks and was now staring in bewilderment. He was fixated on Burk, who had just taken off his undershirt to expose the full extent of his injuries. A ghastly gash ran from Burk's neckline to waistline that bore a resemblance to that on his face, yet was far more pronounced. In fact, the scar looked nothing like a scar at all. If Burk had been bleeding or shown signs of pain, Sky would have assumed the injury had only happened moments prior, as the flesh glowed a dull red and even appeared to be pulsating.

"Ahem." Burk coughed impatiently, trying to regain Sky's attention. "You seem to be lost, so I'll ask you again. What do you think I mean by *situation*?"

Sky shook his head, clearing the image of Burk's injury from his mind. "You mean deal with whoever is causing the ripples?" asked Sky, refusing to look up from the floor as he responded.

"*Deal* is a bit brash," replied Burk, pulling a button down over his torso to Sky's relief. "It depends on the situation. It's important you know this next bit. Keep getting dressed and pay close attention.

"If the source of the ripple ends up being a person, or potentially multiple people for that matter, then we have to use our discretion. If they come from after the Collision, then it could be any number of things that brought them to the Past, but the underlying factor for those types of blokes is they likely won't be happy to be found...and they could be dangerous. If that happens to be the case, we bring them in or take them down. If they're classified B.C., well, they won't have a clue who we are or what the hell's going on. We observe from a distance, approach cautiously, keep them calm, and convince them to come with us quietly if need be."

"And if they *don't* come with us quietly?" asked Sky.

"We do everything in our power to contain them," said Burk sternly. "It's rare for a Pasty to gain abilities. They can be quite powerful though, once we bring them to the Present, depending on how far along they are, that is. As you can imagine, they can be tremendous assets for the Commission."

"And if we *can't* contain them?" asked Sky, with a crooked smile.

Burk paused, taking a moment for silence to fill the room before answering. "Now listen here, *child*, and listen well," said Burk to Sky with authority. "Regardless of what happens out there, you *will* follow my lead. Any sign of you taking matters into your own hands, and—"

"And what?" remarked Sky boldly. "Honestly, Burk, the threats really are getting old. You should at least try to come up with something new to say, you know? Keep things interesting."

Burk made one lengthy step and positioned himself right in front of Sky. He looked down at the recruit in maddened amusement. Sky cocked his head back, looking up to return the favor, challenging the seasoned veteran of the Commission with a smug smile and unfounded bravery.

"We'll see how you handle yourself when the time comes," growled Burk before reaching across the table, causing Sky to flinch. Uniforms in hand, Burk smiled at Sky and shoved a pile of worn clothing into the young man's chest, demanding he place them in the locker and close it shut. Sky obeyed, returning from the locker to see his newly gotten effects laid upon the floor. He huffed in annoyance, placed them in his bag, and took his place near Burk beside the terminal.

Burk fiddled with the terminal screen. This time, when the floor rumbled, it wasn't because they were moving upward. The lockers in front of them began folding inward as each column collapsed on the next, creating a gap large enough for the men to walk through. Burk strutted towards the lockers as they settled and made his way towards the lit entrance, Sky following in his footsteps.

"Alright then chums," said Burk, nodding towards two Commission officers stationed at the front of the bleached room. Much like the one they had left, this room was also fashioned in a circle, but far cozier in terms of its dimensions. Every inch of the walls was covered in holographic monitors, each displaying data related to various points in the Past–all dated around 200 B.C. from what Burk could tell. One of the guards stood beside a raised platform in the very center of the room, surrounded by crescent guardrails, while the other waited just inside folding doors. Both officers were dressed in white from head to toe, aside from the reflective material that covered the top half of their face, stemming from the edge of their protective headwear.

"Papers then," said the nearest female officer, extending her hand out in their direction. Burk took the manila envelope tucked under his arm and pulled out a singular piece of paper. He handed it to the guard, then stuck the envelope back in his bag.

"You too," she said, extending a hand towards Sky.

"Right," said Sky, fiddling around in his bag to find his packet. After an inordinate amount of fidgeting, he pulled the packet from the bag and handed it to her in its entirety. Irritated, the guard took out a single piece of paper, then shoved the envelope back into Sky's chest. Burk chuckled in amusement.

"To the center then," she said, motioning Sky and Burk towards the middle of the room and heading back to the terminal. "Give our man over there a signal when you're ready." The other officer in the room nodded their way, directing Sky and Burk to take their positions in the circle.

"Load up your chrys," said Burk to Sky, taking the purple microchip he had gathered from the locker and sliding it into his compass, "and don't mess about son. If you crack it, I'm not bringing you back with me."

Sky took out his chip and loaded it into the open slit on the end of his compass. He felt a tingling sensation over his body as the screen shined and chimed, showing the device had been loaded with chrys. The tingling subsided in short bursts as the device powered down into standby mode.

"How close will we get?" asked Burk to the officer behind the terminal.

"Pretty accurate, this rig," she replied, half paying attention to him as she dragged projections of data points and strings of code across the holographic monitors. "A little outdated, as I'm sure you can tell, but you'll be as close to the ripple as we can drop you with time to spare...more than a tick, but close nonetheless."

Burk nodded at the female officer and turned back to Sky.

"Ready then?" asked Burk. Sky nodded in approval.

"Send us through," said Burk, nodding to the male officer.

"Hang tight, gents," said the female officer, poking the first of many discrete spherical projections floating in a row as they turned from red to green in sequence, "sending them off in..."

The guardrails around Burk and Sky buzzed.

"Ten...nine... eight..."

The countdown began; sparks darted across the metallic lining of the rails, leaving behind a glittering trail of purple dust.

"Seven...six... five..."

The male officer took a step back and poked at his compass, then crossed his arms and looked towards the center of the room.

"Four...three... two..."

Burk put his glasses on and placed a hand on Sky's shoulder. They both looked up at the guard as he extended his right arm out in their direction, his palm flat, as if giving the men a direction to stop.

"One...zero..."

Sparks shot upwards and outwards towards the center of the room like fireworks, engulfing Sky and Burk in an instant before dissipating. A mere wisp of purple dust floated through the air, taking residence on the floor of the now deserted platform in the center of the circular room.

Z.S. JOSEPH

9.
MUCH ADO ABOUT ICE CREAM

Upon seeing him up close for the first time, Addy understood why he had caused such a commotion. The right side of the man's face was horribly disfigured. Wounded, it seemed, from a knife or a blade that had carved its way through the man's eye and down towards his beard. Addy stared onward as Eli turned to face her, found himself speechless, then turned back towards the man.

"Here you are then, sir," said the parlor clerk from behind the counter, handing the beastly figure a waffle cone brimming with chocolate ice cream covered in sprinkles.

"Much obliged," the man replied, taking the ice cream in one hand and handing money to the clerk with the other. "Keep the change."

Suspended in disbelief, Eli and Addy hadn't noticed that it was Luka the man was handing the ice cream cone to. The man knelt down onto one knee to meet Luka, who graciously accepted his reward, unfazed by the man's horrendous appearance.

"There you are, son," said the man, patting Luka once on the back.

"Thanks very much," said Luka, wasting no time to dig into his tasty treat.

"Ah," said the bearded man, looking in Addy and Eli's direction, "and here must be your compatriots." Luka, captivated by his dessert, nodded in validation. The scar-riddled man got back to his feet, ushering Luka along to meet Addy and Eli, both standing slack-jawed at the entrance of the store.

"Ahem," coughed the man, politely breaking the silence. "Apologies. A bit unorthodox I'm sure, but your friend here ran into the store and was rudely cut in line. He was so excited, I offered him to join me at the front, and I insisted on purchasing his cone."

"Thanks," responded Addy, first to come to her senses. "You didn't have to do that."

"No trouble at all. You have yourselves a polite little gentleman there."

Luka beamed up at them, chocolate ice cream splattered across his face, trickling and staining the front of his shirt. Seeing this, the tall man let out a hearty chuckle.

"Luka, how about you get some napkins and save us a

table outside," said Eli, forcing a smile towards his brother. "Meet you out there in a pip."

Luka shrugged and skipped his way past Addy and Eli towards the back of the parlor.

"Apologies, I've had the pleasure of meeting Luka, but I haven't gotten your names," said the man.

"Sorry, I'm Addy–this is Eli," she said reluctantly.

"Yes, Eli Smith," he said, reaching out to the tall man for a handshake. "Luka is my younger brother."

"Ah," breathed the tall man observingly, firmly shaking Eli's hand in kind. "A couple of gentlemen, I see. Your parents must be proud."

"I see you didn't buy anything," interjected Addy.

"Yes," replied the man. "Very observant, Addy. I had finished my order just before Luka arrived and as fate would have it, we bumped into one another before I was able to depart."

"You look dry," retorted Addy. "Didn't I see you out in the rain?"

"Spot on again, Addy. Sharp as a tack, I see," responded the man. "I was lucky enough to get inside shortly after the rain had started. I took respite in this establishment and decided while I was here, I may as well test the parlor's goods."

Addy raised an eyebrow.

"Well, I must be off," said the man rather abruptly. "It was lovely to meet the both of you. I do hope that our paths cross again." He took the glasses from his breast pocket, slid them on, then made for the door.

"Good day, Addy and Eli," said the tall man as he exited the parlor.

"Nice bloke," said Eli to Addy. "See? Nothing to worry about."

"Eli, don't you think it's a bit odd for someone like that to buy a little boy ice cream?" asked Addy.

"I mean, if he was luring him towards a van, maybe," joked Eli. "But it's not like he was in here alone. I think he was just being nice. You saw him–I'm sure loads of people treat him poorly all the time, being all 'judgey' and whatnot. He probably welcomed the company of someone that wasn't horrified by the massive gash on his face."

Addy gulped at the thought of who or what could have caused an injury to a man like that. "Still," she implored, "think about it. A ton of people probably rushed in here during the storm. Even if he did come in, stand in line, eat, and run into Luka, there's no way he'd be bone dry by now, right?"

"I don't know, Addy," griped Eli. "You're thinking about it too much. Maybe he dried himself off in the back."

"With what? Do they have blow-dryers in the back?" asked Addy. "We're in an ice cream parlor, not a salon. It makes no sense. There's no way he could look like that after sitting out in the rain."

"His clothes are probably water resistant. Honestly, Ads, I don't know," admitted Eli. "Look, we found your man, and he was a nice bloke. Admittedly quite odd looking, but nice. And to top it off, he paid for Luka's ice cream, so he's alright in my book. Yeah?"

They stood in line and waited in silence until they reached the counter. Eli ordered a large hot fudge sundae in a bowl. The clerk pulled his order together, then turned towards Addy to ask what he could get for her.

"That man from before," said Addy to the clerk. "The tall man with the cap. I'll have what he had."

"What? You mean the bloke with the scar?" asked the clerk. "He ordered a chocolate ice cream with sprinkles for the kid. Is that what you want, miss?"

"He didn't order anything for himself?" asked Addy.

"No, miss, just the one cone."

Addy eye's shot daggers in Eli's direction. Eli, entranced by his mountain of ice cream, didn't take notice. Annoyed, Addy turned and ordered herself a strawberry ice cream in a sugar cone from the clerk. Eli paid for them both, pausing long enough to hand money over before shoveling another whopping scoop of fudge into his mouth.

Once they'd finally made it to the back of the parlor, which took quite some time as Eli paused and took a bite with every other step, Addy opened the door for Eli, allowing him to pass through, his hands preoccupied with his sundae.

They stepped out onto a quaint wooden patio, strung with lights that twinkled even in the daylight. Black bistro tables, each surrounded by four chairs, were stationed in each corner with pools of water filling each seat's crescent basin. The patio itself extended out to the edge of the now busy sidewalk.

It didn't take long for them to find Luka. He was standing in the middle of the patio, facing a rotund boy wearing a white shirt that scarcely covered his belly. The front of the boy's shirt was no longer white, as it had been stained with a marshy brown blob that had formed from an amalgam of different ice cream flavors and toppings. Alongside the boy stood a lanky woman with skin that looked of leather, brought about from a lifetime dedicated to the tanning booth. She wore an all-white outfit, complete with a tennis hat and a tautly pulled ponytail.

Addy and Eli glared in disappointment, at once recognizing the pair standing before Luka. The chunky boy, Stewart, and his mother, Guinevere, were no strangers to their families. Prue and Magnus worked together year round on their shared farmstead, growing an assortment of crops, fruits, and vegetables, and breeding select livestock. At the market where they would often peddle their goods, Guinevere always had some issue or another with what they were selling. Most recently, she had gone so far as to file a complaint with the local regulators, claiming that Magnus and Prue were selling yellow zucchinis that were unorthodox and not up to code. After the regulator's quick inspection, followed by a private discussion with Guinevere, they were able to convince her that the plant itself was, in fact, a squash.

"I saw you do it!" snapped Guinevere, putting her finger in Luka's face.

"Hey!" yelled Addy, furious to see how close Guinevere was to touching Luka and rushing to his aid.

"Oh, here we go," groaned Eli with a mouth full of ice cream. He dropped his sundae on a nearby table, catching up to Addy as she rushed towards Guinevere.

"What's going on here, Guinevere?" asked Addy, trying to remain as calm as possible.

"That'll be Mrs. Linden to you," growled Guinevere, looking Addy up and down with contempt.

"Hi, Mrs. Linden," interjected Eli, "how are you today?"

Guinevere turned to face Eli and inspected him even more closely than she had Addy.

"Ah, Eli," said Guinevere, "that little brother of yours walked right up to my Stewart and smacked an ice cream cone right out of his hands!"

"I didn't, Eli, I swear," implored Luka, "he took my ice cream from me and started eating it. I tried to get it back, but he dropped his and mine on the ground." Luka stared down at the floor where a pool of chocolate ice cream lay melting next to half eaten piles of vanilla, strawberry, and cake batter. Each of the four distinct colors was smeared across Stewart's face and down the front of his overburdened shirt.

"You filthy little liar. My Stewart would never do such a thing!" gasped Guinevere.

"Filthy!?" said Addy, fuming at Guinevere's response.

"Alright, alright," reassured Eli, "let's all calm down. We'll get you a new scoop of ice cream, alright Luka?"

"And what about Stewart?" asked Guinevere. "I expect he'll be given a replacement cone to compensate for Luka bullying my son."

"I think we can all agree that he doesn't exactly *need* any more ice cream," said Addy heatedly. Guinevere's jaw dropped. Stewart's eyes watered, then streamed down from his face. He looked up at the sky and whined inconsolably.

"You–you little tramp!" bellowed Guinevere. "How *dare* you call my son fat!"

"I didn't call him fat, did I?" asked Addy smugly. "Those were your words, Mrs. Linden, not mine."

Guinevere's face flushed. Her skin transformed from leathery-orange to bright red. She tilted her head back in a fit of rage and took a deep breath, preparing to unleash a verbal assault.

"You little SHIT!" shrieked Guinevere, taken aback and grasping her sobbing son in a protective stance. She moved in front of Stewart, then stepped forward to be as near to Addy as possible without touching her. Addy winced at the smell of Guinevere's breath.

"Who told you that you could talk to me like that?" shouted Guinevere. "You disrespectful, filthy, good-for-nothing—"

Guinevere yelled every insult she could think of, struggling at times to form actual words in her enraged state. The commotion attracted the attention of passersby on the sidewalk, who quickened their pace to escape the sounds of the madwoman bellowing at the top of her lungs and the deafening cries of her obese child.

Addy was so taken aback by both Stewart and Guinevere she could barely believe the scene unfolding before her was actually happening. Luka stood nearby and covered his ears, shielding himself from the sounds of Stewart's sharp shrieks and Guinevere's frustrated screaming. Eli furrowed his brow and took in the scene, wincing as he panned across Stewart and Guinevere. He looked down at Luka, placing his hands over his brother's ears to deafen the cacophony of sounds. He then turned back towards Addy; his face painted with disappointment.

Addy caught a glimpse of Eli, and the look he gave was enough for her to question if she'd gone overboard by dragging Guinevere's son into the crossfire. Still, she refused to feel guilty. The Linden's had done far worse than she–the years of unnecessary obstacles Guinevere had placed upon her family and friends, going out of her way to slight and belittle them at every opportunity. Not to mention the bullying Stewart had imposed upon Luka that occurred without repercussion. Guinevere was dependably stubborn in her defense of Stewart and his ability to do no wrong, and Addy had had enough.

"Are you even *listening* to me!?" squawked Guinevere. Addy's lack of response infuriated Guinevere, who had grown accustomed to people kowtowing to her every whim.

Frustrated, Guinevere took her pointer finger and took aim, jabbing Addy in her sternum repeatedly.

"Are–you–list–en–ing–to–me?" repeated Guinevere, stabbing Addy with her finger between each syllable.

"Ouch—" uttered Addy, shoving Guinevere's hand away from her forcefully.

"Hey!" blurted a stunned Eli. "There's no need for that!"

Guinevere took a step back, grasping the wrist that Addy had pushed away and casting an evil grin. She scrunched her face and looked back at Addy and Eli, ensuring they took notice.

"Assault!" hollered Guinevere, "Please! Help! Assault!"

Her cries for help worked, catching the attention of onlookers. A couple stopped to stare in confusion. Two children stopped to look on, prompting their mother and father to take notice. A slender woman wrestled to restrain her Bullmastiff, who began yanking on his leash and barking in Guinevere's direction. A small crowd formed as gawkers huddled together on the sidewalk, wishing to themselves that someone would have the stomach to jump in and help. Stewart noticed the crowd and elevated his cries, working hard to play his part as an innocent victim.

"Assault!?" laughed Addy, shocked by the lengths Guinevere would go. "You put your hands on me first!"

"Mrs. Linden, please," implored Eli, "is all of this necessary?"

"Assault!" yelled Guinevere, ignoring the two completely.

The nearby crowd amassed further. Guinevere's voice and Stewart's cries attracted looky-loos like moths to a flame.

"Alright, alright. Settle down, everyone," a person yelled sternly from the edge of the sidewalk. "Step aside, step aside." The crowd sighed with relief and acknowledged the request, parting down the middle to make way for a police officer to pass through their ranks.

"Alright, ma'am," said the officer to Guinevere, "what seems to be the problem?"

"Them!" she quivered, pointing a shaky hand in their direction. Addy tried to cut in and explain how the situation unfolded but was cut off by Guinevere, clutching her wrist in apparent agony, begging the officer to let her tell her side of the story.

"Go on then, ma'am," said the officer to Guinevere.

"Take it easy, Ads," whispered Eli in Addy's ear as Guinevere told her tall tale to the officer, opening with the bold claim that Addy and Luka had accosted her and her son both verbally and physically, fabricating every instance of the story in her favor.

"Hey! Those're the dustbin lids that were mucking about in my shop!" said a familiar voice from the crowd. "Telling porky pies, no doubt–Adam and Eve me."

"Why, yes! Those are the children that left my beautiful boutique in *ruins*!" sang another voice from the front, the word 'ruins' rolling off her fiery tongue and stirring up the rabble.

Addy felt helpless. Unable to defend herself or her friends, her frustration transformed into boiling anger. She balled each of her hands into a fist at her sides, clenching them fiercely. She felt extremely hot, burning from the inside out, kindled by her rage.

"Oh, shut up you wench!" roared Addy.

"Ads," warned Eli, reaching out to place a hand on her shoulder.

"No," replied a disillusioned Addy, batting him away. "She's *lying* through her crooked teeth." Addy turned to face the police officer. Their eyes connected, and Addy prayed the lawman would recognize the pain in her eyes. The officer took the poor girl in. His jaw set, and he nodded in Addy's direction.

Addy frantically recounted every detail of the story to the officer. "Please believe me," she continued, "we have a history with this woman. She's had it out for us for years, and today's no different. And if you don't believe me, well fine! Have it your way." Addy paused for a moment and breathed deeply. She looked over at her friends and sighed, then turned back to the officer. "But please, don't blame these two," said Addy, motioning to Luka and Eli. "It's not their fault."

"Ah–see? A confession then!" snarled Guinevere. "Officer, perhaps it's best I have a word with you in private?" she insisted, pulling Stewart back towards the parlor. The officer sighed and told Addy, Eli, and Luka to stay put, turned on his heel, and went to meet Guinevere and her son in the ice cream parlor.

Addy, still fuming, turned her back to Eli and Luka and gazed into the crowd. She opened her mouth to tell them off when she became fixated on a figure separated from the crowd. She had once again spotted the tall, scarred man who stood still, hands in his pockets, fixated on her location. Addy cocked her head and stared back at him. The parlor's back door flew open, and Addy broke her trance to turn and see the officer exiting the parlor with Guinevere and Stewart following a short distance behind him.

"Look," sighed the officer as he approached Addy. He removed his Sillito cap, placed it under his arm, wiped the sweat off his brow with the opposite hand, and looked at her sincerely. "There isn't much I can do here. Your–er–acquaintance, Mrs. Linden, has shared she'd like to press charges."

"What!?" uttered Addy incredulously.

"You can't be serious," remarked Eli in a similar tone. "There has to be someone here who can corroborate our story. Addy was only defending herself."

"Look," repeated the officer. "You may not like it, but we *can* avoid all this. Mrs. Linden has agreed that if you apologize and compensate her son, she will consider not pursuing this matter further."

Addy and Eli gaped at the officer in disbelief.

"Look", sighed the officer again, "I'm sure you don't like it, but I can assure you the alternative will be far worse for all of us. Aside from the pile of paperwork on my end, your troubles will have only begun–the legal fees, the time you'll have to spend dealing with lawyers and the magistrates' court. Those are only a few of the many costly activities you'll have to endure."

Addy and Eli stared back with blank faces; the officer leaned in, whispering so that only Addy and Eli alone could hear.

"And if I were you, I'd give the old bat what she wants and get yourselves out of here. Between us, we all know she's a bit mental, but she's got the time and the means to make this a real problem."

Addy shifted her gaze from the officer to Guinevere and Stewart, who were adorned with smug looks. Addy's rage sweltered and boiled over. *No, they can't get away with this*, she thought, clenching her hands into fists of fury.

"Let it go, Ads," muttered Eli. "Right then, we'll do that," he continued graciously to the officer. "Thanks for your help, sir."

"I'm not apologizing," said Addy through grit teeth, "I won't do it."

"If we pay for the ice cream, will that be enough?" begged Eli.

The officer's face sank. "Let me see what I can do."

Addy looked past the officer at her sworn enemies. Guinevere and Stewart stared back–Guinevere's face contorted into a twisted smile and Stewart stuck his tongue out. The officer turned to face them. Guinevere and Stewart wiped the looks from their faces before the officer could take notice.

"Well? What'll it be, ma'am?" asked the officer to Guinevere.

Guinevere held back a response, taking the time to leer at the trio, casting her left eyebrow up high. "Given the way they were raised, I suppose I shouldn't have expected anything less," said Guinevere disappointedly to the officer. "Yes, I suppose, for today, that will do."

"I'm sorry, Addy," said Luka. His lips quivered, and he grabbed Addy's hand and squeezed it tight. The act kept Addy's anger at bay. Addy sighed and pulled Luka towards her. The troubled boy drew near and hugged her at the waist. Addy looked down at Luka, hugging him with one arm at the shoulder. She looked up and her eyes met Guinevere's, the two glaring at one another in defiance.

Z.S. JOSEPH

10.
STEP 1: DETECT

Sky blinked uncontrollably, partially blinded by the seared image of lightning rods that had overtaken him and Burk moments prior. He looked around, turning right to left, then left to right, desperate to determine where he'd been Pushed.

"Burk? Burk! Are you there?" yelled Sky.

"Calm down, son," replied Burk, "over here."

"I can't see a damn thing!" said Sky, spinning around, looking hopelessly to find the direction of Burk's voice.

"Give it a moment, it'll pass," said Burk calmly. "Next time, you might want to put your oculars on before a big Push. But I suppose you knew that along with the rest of the basics, eh?"

"You bastard! My eyes are *burning!* Why didn't you tell me?" Sky rubbed his eyes in desperation, opened them as wide as possible, then started rubbing them again in a panic.

"Keep your voice down," commanded Burk, "close your eyes and give them a rest. It'll come back in a moment."

Sky slammed his eyes shut. The afterimage of sparks lingered amongst the dark backdrop of his eyelids. He took a deep breath, allowing the darkness to overtake the edges of his view as the sparks subsided. He peeled open his eyelids, relieved to find his vision inching back at the peripherals.

"You alright then?" asked Burk.

"I can *barely* see," snapped Sky.

"But you can see? Good enough. You'll be right as rain in no time. Now follow me and keep quiet," said Burk with a turn.

Burk started off slowly, making it easier for Sky to follow. Sky, able to see just enough of the ground and Burk's feet to keep up, remained vigilant as they moved through the densely wooded area. He moved cautiously, muttering empty threats about what he would do to Burk once his vision returned to normal.

While Sky's sense of sight was still coming to, his other senses were working in overdrive. The cracking of dried leaves and twigs boomed in his ears with each step. Further along, Sky noticed he felt much lighter. Taking a deep breath, he found the air to be crisp and much cleaner than what he was used to. His movements seemed trivial, as though they took little to no effort at all.

"So...where did they Push us to, exactly?" asked Sky.

"Ah, so you know what a Push is then, do you?"

"Went on a few trips to the Past with my parents when I was a kid. We never traveled back quite like that, though."

"Traveled in style then, I presume. The 'when' I've already told you–around 200 B.C.–the 'where' I'm getting a lock on now," continued Burk. "The report said we'd be traveling to the West–somewhere in Europe. As far as I can tell, we're zeroing in on a few probable locations, likely one of the larger islands."

After walking for a quarter of an hour, Sky and Burk came upon a clearing. "Pretty accurate, my arse," muttered Burk to himself. He crouched and turned to Sky, signaling him to keep quiet and follow with caution. Sky, whose vision had almost fully recovered, nodded in confirmation. He crouched down to stay hidden–though from what he wasn't sure–and followed Burk, creeping along at a snail's pace. The men halted just before the trunk of a downed tree. Burk rested his bag aside the tree's wide and tarnished trunk and took a knee.

Beyond the woods, the men saw two old brick houses that seemed identical to one another. In front of the houses, a grassy lawn extended out to a short wooden fence–the lawn itself divided in two by a dirt road. The road came to a path that lay between the houses, continuing to a silver, domelike barn, double the height and triple the width of each house.

"This is it," whispered Burk, "The likely location of the ripple. We're a bit early. Put your oculars on. You'll need to sync them up with your compass. Start scanning the area–look for signatures of chrys."

Sky whipped a pair of oculars out of his bag and put them

on. He rolled up his sleeve to expose the compass that had just been lashed to his left arm, keying in the command to take the device out of standby mode. Immediately, a rush of euphoria overcame him, coursing throughout his entire body before settling into a sensation of coolness that felt like the first breeze of spring.

Sky looked down at the compass again in awe–his exposed arm was glowing purple. He held his hand to his face, mesmerized by the sight as his hand gleamed like a small purple sun, emitting miniature coronal flares as he wiggled his fingers. He looked back at the controls on his compass, eager to see what else the device had in store for him. An image of sunglasses rotating in the center of a dotted circle flashed on the screen. Sky pressed it, and a new screen popped up, allowing him to select from a listing of different functions for his oculars. He pressed another dotted circle with the image of a purple crystal spinning in the center. His oculars darkened at once, obscuring his vision to the degree he found himself in when they'd arrived on the scene.

"Well, this is funny, isn't it?" said Sky with an undertone of annoyance, taking his oculars off to look at Burk. "I can't see a damned thing now."

"Shh–keep it down. Look around and try to find a trace. Start with the sky, Sky," chuckled Burk as he pointed upwards.

"Satisfied with yourself on that one?" groaned Sky. He motioned to replace his oculars and looked up, frozen. "The sky here is so...blue. Where did you say we were again?"

"Put your ocs back on and–help–me–look," said Burk through a clenched jaw.

Sky obeyed, putting his oculars on to look back into the void. He looked down at his monitor, which glowed through the darkness, and selected a secondary mode that allowed him to zoom in and out. Sky experimented with the device's settings, trying out one function after another, giving up after peering into the darkness for the better part of five minutes.

"This is boring," said Sky, removing his oculars. "I'm bored again."

"Look around the houses," said Burk, ignoring Sky's remarks. "Same setting. Search for traces of chrys or any signs of life."

Sky rolled his eyes so that Burk couldn't see, then put his oculars back on again to look forward. "Wait…signs of life?" asked Sky, his brain working in overdrive. "Does that mean there are Pasties here that caused the ripples?"

Burk let out a heavy sigh. "It's possible, but it's more likely that some sort of cosmic signatures traced their way back to this location. Happens all the time, us finding them around people in the Past. The world was more densely populated during this time than it is in the Present, and there's less interference in the atmosphere. Now, keep your eyes forward, and let me know if you see anything."

Sky acted like he'd accepted Burk's explanation, but Burk knew better. What he omitted to tell the recruit was that it was unusual for the ripple to trace itself back to a remote location with so few people present. Not *impossible*, Burk thought, but far less likely. Would he really have to work with Sky to contain the situation, or worse yet, contain Sky? A situation far beyond what he had bargained for, and one that would likely not bode well for him or the Commission.

Burk switched his settings to thermal, adjusting his field of view to reveal the houses and front lawn in their entirety. He focused his attention on the leftmost house. As he closed in, three figures took form—two females in separate rooms and one four-legged creature somewhere between them. He panned to the next house on the right and located two males—one motionless in a slouched position, the other inching across the front room of the house.

Burk scaled the view of the oculars back to get another look at the collective perimeter of the houses. Immediately, his eyes darted back to the front lawn of the leftmost house. The flash of another unexpected heat signature caught his eye. He zoomed back in to see the outline of a small boy lying on the front lawn.

Burk furrowed his brow and looked down at his monitor. They were still in range of the ripple, but on which side of it, he couldn't tell. *That child must have been there before*, thought Burk, *must've missed the little lad the first time, that's all.*

"Do you see anything?" asked Burk calmly, not wanting to raise Sky's suspicions.

"Why yes, Burk," said Sky dryly, causing Burk's ears to

perk and his heart to flutter. "Yes, I see a unicorn, and a dancing elf, and a–*ow–ow–ow*!"

Burk pulled on Sky's ear, punishing him as he would a misbehaving child. "Tell me what you see," demanded Burk through a clenched jaw.

"Alright, alright–let go of me!" begged Sky as Burk released him from his clutches. "I see the same exact thing I've seen since I started looking through these ridiculous things, which just so happens to be *absolutely nothing*."

Burk let out a sigh, relieved to hear that Sky had said nothing about the boy. Had he done or mentioned anything out of the ordinary, it might mean he'd have an actual situation on his hands, especially with Sky in his presence. It hadn't solved everything though, as Burk wasn't convinced the boy had been there the whole time. But if not, how had he gotten there undetected?

"Glad to see you're taking this seriously," said Burk, "I thought you'd be grateful, not being cooped up in another Commission classroom."

"Yeah, it's been a real treat so far," said Sky, rubbing his ear and looking vacantly through his oculars.

The front door of the rightmost house whispered open. The act didn't go unnoticed by Sky. His auditory senses were still in overdrive, causing him to strain in discomfort as the sound echoed in his ears like nails on a chalkboard.

"Wait," said Sky through a wince. "I think I see something.

It's like a–a dark blob. It's floating across the front of the house over there."

Burk looked over and caught the thermal image of one of the larger males, changed the setting of his oculars, and looked up. The male figure had been replaced by a ghostly essence, indistinguishable in form and only a shade lighter than the otherwise sea of darkness.

"He's an Aug then, yeah?" asked Sky to Burk's surprise.

"Again, it's possible," said Burk.

"Well, if anyone should know about Augs—"

"Best to not make any hasty conclusions," surmised Burk. "His signature's so low that it's hardly registering. It's highly improbable he's the cause of what we're here to find."

"Still, we need to monitor them, don't we?" asked Sky knowingly.

"Augs? Yes, and no. Yes, in that we need to find out if they have any augmentations, but we are not to engage otherwise. It's not uncommon for Pasties to have the inherent characteristics of an Aug, but we can't assume that they're from the Present. If we detect any implants or see him use any uncommon abilities for this time, we'll know for sure," said Burk, switching the setting on his oculars. The enhanced view through his black spectacles was now more akin to looking through a giant magnifying glass. He was observing with perfect clarity the figures on the lawn, just in time to catch the face of a third female figure joining them.

Sky and Burk continued to observe while the three figures

conversed before the two males took their leave. Burk traced their path until they escaped his direct view by entering the rightmost house, then panned back to see the face of the female, squinting at him as though face-to-face through his enhanced view.

"What the–shit!" exclaimed Burk, grabbing Sky by the collar. He Jumped, and they vanished, reappearing behind the tree line amongst the heavy woods from where they'd entered.

"You've got to be careful with that setting when we're observing," said Burk, "these're an older model. The lenses glow red when you scan for chrys. Helps block out some of the interference."

"Let me guess–I would have known that, had I studied more," said Sky. Burk ignored the comment and walked cautiously back in the direction of the houses.

The men made it through the woods to their previous rally point, displacing to take a new position in a location with far better coverage to avoid being compromised. Burk directed Sky with hand gestures, all of which, to Burk's surprise, Sky knew. They waited and continued to survey the scene for about an hour, during which time Sky reminded Burk that he was bored at least a dozen times, before one of the older males, the boy, and the younger of the two females regrouped at the truck parked between the houses.

"Listen," said Burk, "I'm going to tail that lot and see if I can find anything. You stay here and keep an eye on things. Keep your distance, and *do not* engage while I'm away. If anything happens, Jolt your way back into the woods. I'll trace your signature on my compass."

"You can't be serious," replied Sky dubiously. "Nothing's happened since we've got here. Can't I go and you stay here?"

Burk shot him a weighty look, enough for Sky to get the message. The truck pulled out onto the dirt road and puttered by them noisily while they remained undetected.

"Like I said, stay hidden, and *do not* engage," said Burk. He stood up and looked down the road until the truck was only just visible and Jumped, leaving Sky all by himself.

"Well, this is boring," sighed Sky. "Hopefully these two will do something interesting," he said to himself, looking onward at the remaining female figure as she crossed the dirt path to meet the remaining male who sat and smoked on the front patio.

II.

BRAIN FREEZE

Addy, Eli, and Luka exited the marketplace and returned to their defeated-looking truck, mirroring how they all felt on the inside. Cramped together on the front bench, Luka squeezed himself between Addy and Eli. His eyes welled up, and he leaned towards Addy, shoving his face into her shoulder. Addy squeezed the boy, and he returned the gesture tenfold.

"I'm sorry, Addy," said Luka.

"Don't be sorry," said Addy, pulling him back to look the boy in his eyes. "You did nothing wrong. Never say sorry if you didn't do something wrong."

"But I've gone and ruined your birthday, haven't I?" replied Luka, head sunken toward the floor.

"You did no such thing!" said Addy assuredly, leaning

back to look at the boy directly. "I had a wonderful day, all thanks to you."

Luka sniffed his nose and looked back up at Addy.

"Don't worry about that old hag or her portly pig of a son. Some people are just, well, awful. But you can't let them get to you, Luka. That's what they want. You let them do that, then they've already won. Right?"

Luka nodded at her in agreement. Addy spoke with conviction, yet the words held little merit to her in the present moment. She believed the advice she'd shared with Luka, but she was still furious at the injustice she'd just been served. She recalled Eli surrendering a heaping ice cream cone over to Stewart and the subsequent look that Guinevere gave her. The image was seared into her memory–Guinevere's leathery face lathered with malicious glee, the narrowing of her overly groomed brow, her inflated lips pressing together, contorting into a wicked sneer. Once again, Addy felt anger and frustration, brought about by the arrogance of Guinevere, who had a knack for causing her blood to boil.

"But what about the policeman? He still made us pay for a new ice cream cone," said Luka.

"He wasn't a bad man," interjected Eli, "he was in a tough spot, you know? Personally, I don't agree with his decision, but in the end, he did help us out in a way."

"How?" asked Luka. Addy glared at Eli.

"It's–er–complicated," replied Eli. "You'll understand when you're older."

Eli cleared his throat, stifling a cough. Addy stared at Eli incredulously. He pretended not to see her, grasping the wheel as the truck bounced along the bumpy road.

Oh, I swear to God if Luka wasn't in this truck right now, Addy thought, her imagination getting the better of her.

"If you say so," said Luka drowsily. With his conscience clear and the day's events giving way to exhaustion, he let out a deep yawn. He grasped Addy by the arm and leaned his head against her. "Happy Birthday," he whispered before he closed his eyes, let out a deep sigh, and drifted to sleep.

Addy and Eli sat in silence, the sound of occasional rumblings from the truck's undercarriage being the only sound of respite from an otherwise deafening silence. Addy brooded over recent events, glaring at Eli intermittently, shooting daggers in his direction that he plainly ignored. She replayed the scene with Guinevere over and over, eventually accepting there was nothing she could do about it now. Justice would be served and, while that day may not be today, she promised herself that when the day came, she would be the one to serve it.

However, as comforting as that realization may be, it did not lift Addy's spirits entirely. Sure, Guinevere would get hers, but today's events left her sour towards Eli as well. Addy knew she was being irrational, thinking that Eli had given in to Guinevere's demands without hesitation. Eli had been tactful, shielding both her and Luka from the possibility of a more explosive situation. Still, Addy wished Eli had, for once, grown a spine and chosen a more direct approach over some form of casual diplomacy. And if he wouldn't come to her aid on her birthday of all days, then when?

Addy shook her head, trying to cast out the selfish thoughts brewing in her mind. Eli had her back, she knew. Even if she was *sometimes* in the wrong. Even if she did not always agree with the way Eli handled things. He was always there for her and Luka. No matter what, he had her back.

What about the scarred man? The thought crept its way past the wall of assurance she'd been constructing in her mind. She flashed back to the image of the man, staring back at her, looking on in her time of need. Eli didn't seem to have her back on that one, at least for most of the day, did he?

Stop it, she thought to herself. Still, at minimum, there was something odd about the man. Regardless of how Eli had tried to play it, deep down, she still believed the man had been hiding something from them. To what end, she hadn't a clue, but her gut instinct told her there was more to the story.

Deep in thought, Addy cranked her window down, enough to take in a cool breeze of fresh air. She closed her eyes and leaned against the door, shimmying into a comfortable position. The thoughts in her mind were spinning, and she wanted to relax. Humming a tune to herself to keep busy, she looked down at Luka, who slept peacefully beside her.

Luka, she thought. Her spinning thoughts took form. Luka had been at the ice cream shop with the scarred man before they arrived, she recalled with excitement. She looked back at the boy, eager to pick his brain for more information, before coming to a pause.

He's been through enough today already, she thought. Her urge to wake Luka subsided. Still, when the time was right, and Luka was rested, asking him about the man would be the first thing she'd do.

A long ride ahead, Addy sat back in her seat and got comfortable. She closed her eyes and took in the breeze once more, contemplating what answers Luka would have in store for her. She returned to her humming, creating a harmonious tune between her hums and the vibrations of the truck. Before long, her mind cleared, making room for exhaustion to set it. Addy dropped her head, leaving her thoughts behind, replacing them with a black void.

Z.S. JOSEPH

12.
STEP 2: MONITOR

Burk remained vigilant, yet more relaxed, without Sky lurking in his midst. Despite his preference to not leave the recruit alone, bringing him along the journey was a much riskier decision. He concluded that leaving him behind was a wise decision, as it would prevent him from being exposed to a larger population and more opportunities to cause trouble.

Tailing the truck was a straightforward task for Burk. After making two turns, the truck drove along a straight path, making it that much easier to track. The road was surrounded by trees on either side and devoid of traffic, giving him plenty of cover and little worry as he worked to remain hidden.

Careful to save both time and resources, Burk would take a position amongst the tree line, scan the path ahead to find the furthest point where the truck could either turn or continue its forward trajectory, then Jump to the probable spot that the truck was likely to appear. He'd be sure to Jump ahead of schedule to account for any possible deviations, then he'd repeat the process until the truck reached its destination.

Enduring this repetitive cycle freed Burk's mind to wander. Normally certain of himself in every way, he was still questioning the child on the lawn, and if the boy had truly been there when they arrived. *It would be a miracle for a Pasty that age to cause those ripples*, he thought, *but still... Perhaps now was the right time for a little stress test to see what the boy might be capable of...*

Burk Jumped, further ahead than he'd done before, creating far more time and space between himself and the current location of the truck. He tilted his head back to survey the trees, then Jumped again, disappearing in an instant from his place on the ground and reappearing amongst the stems and leaves above. He perched upon a branch that he deemed sturdy enough to hold his weight. Balancing himself against the tree's trunk, he raised a knee to his chest, then slammed his leg down and out towards the branch's center, driving his foot cleanly through it. The branch plummeted to the ground, and he Jumped beneath it, appearing with plenty of time to catch the mass of lumber on his shoulder, handling it as though weightless.

Stationed near the side of the road, Burk looked to the truck in the distance, calculating its speed to inform him of his next maneuver. As the truck closed in, he bent into a low runner starting position, grasping the branch with one hand, adjusting the settings of his oculars with the other.

The truck closed in, and he made two successive Jumps, leaving the branch in the middle of the road with the first, turning to observe their reaction from the opposite side of the road with the second, the act completely undetectable by the untrained eye.

The driver swerved at the last second, avoiding the obstruction in the road by a hair. The rear of the truck skidded back and forth–the driver fighting to maintain control. Burk held his breath, hoping that the feeling of imminent danger would trigger something hidden deep within the boy in the truck. He stood at the ready, prepared to make a move should he find that any of the truck's passengers were, in fact, the embodiment of something that was much more than the eye could perceive.

Trailing high on the edge of the road, the truck bed screeched as it swung back onto the main road and found its center. Burk scanned in anticipation for a sign. Aside from the elevation in the passenger's heart rates, no other change in readings was detectable through his oculars.

From that point on, Burk shadowed the truck, running no interference. He kept a safe distance, leaving the passengers to themselves, scanning the truck for signs periodically. The group soon arrived at a small town with a dividing avenue lined with tents and buildings on either side. Once he confirmed the truck had stopped at its intended location–the two males and female having exited the vehicle–Burk rolled his sleeve over his compass, removed his oculars, stepped out from the cover of the woods, and strolled into town, scanning his surroundings for a vantage point to keep a close eye on his targets.

He took his first post outside one of the nearby tents with every intention of blending in. Burk had expertise in conducting recon missions like this, but he admitted it wasn't his forte. Trouble is, Burk's distinct features–tall as a tree, thick as an ox, and horribly disfigured–stuck out like a sore thumb regardless of when and where he went. Unsurprisingly, today was no different, at least in that regard.

Glancing down to check that his monitor was hidden, he noticed a small boy, no older than age five, staring at him in disbelief. Burk turned to the boy, grabbed the bill of his flat cap, put on the friendliest smile he could muster, and gave the boy a nod.

"Hello there, son," said Burk pleasantly. "You lost?"

The boy clamped his jaw shut and welled up. He pursed his lips, trying to hold back tears as they wavered and trembled. The pools of water under his eyes ran over and began spilling onto his cheeks. The boy's mouth dropped open to scream, but no noise came out. He took a deep breath and tried again, letting out a lengthy cry.

"Right," muttered Burk, unsurprised by the boy's reaction. It was not the first time this had happened to Burk, and he was certain it would not be the last. He looked away from the boy, ignoring him to focus on his targets. The child continued to take in large breaths, followed by pitched cries of horror.

"Edward? Edward darling, what's the matter? What

happened?" said a woman's voice concernedly. Edward said nothing and merely pointed in Burk's direction as the woman scooped him up in her arms. "Don't worry, momma's here—shh—momma Hilda's here," said Hilda, hugging her weeping son.

"Excuse me," said Hilda to Burk in an accusatory tone. "What have you done to my son?"

Burk turned his head just enough to see Edward's mother, keeping his targets in his peripheral view. The position he faced gave Hilda a clear view of his scar. She shuddered, attempting to stifle her gasp, but it escaped her, and did not go unnoticed. Burk let out a grunted chuckle, turning his back to Edward and Hilda, and returned his focus back to his intended targets.

"How—how dare you expose my child to—to such hideousness!" stuttered Hilda, embracing Edward, bouncing him in her chest to calm the boy down. "Surely you understand a monster like you should not be allowed around children!"

I don't have time for this, thought Burk, exhaling in annoyance. Edward and his pain for a mother had already stirred up too much attention for Burk's liking. He had his eye on the one female target, who he noticed was now squinting at him with distinct interest.

"Excuse me! Look at me when I'm talking to—"

Hilda's voice was muffled by a sudden and dense wind. She braced herself, clinging to her son, safeguarding the child from being swept away.

Without warning, Burk wrapped his left arm around Hilda, pulling her and Edward inward and spinning to position the three of them between the cover of the now fluttering entranceway of a nearby tent. He looked inside to find an exit exposing covered woods in the distance and Jumped as far back as he could see. The three reappeared amongst the denseness of trees. Burked Jumped twice more, bringing the three of them further and further away from the town. On the third and final Jump, having landed a satisfying distance away, Burk released Hilda and Edward from his captivity.

Edward's mother looked at Burk with a face of complete confusion. Edward, who had stopped crying, gazed at his surroundings in bewilderment. Burk pinched the tip of his cap, nodded to Edward and Hilda with a grin, turned on his heel, then vanished, abandoning them in an open field.

Making his way back to civilization, Burk found himself back at the edge of the woods and, to his luck, found the group he'd been tailing as they exited the back of the first tent. As the group entered the next, Burk made his way back to town, spotted an empty bench in the center avenue enclosed by pristinely pruned bushes, and decided it an adequate position to lie low and track the group without drawing attention or using more chrys than he already had.

Sitting down, Burk took a moment to glance at his compass. He crumpled and straightened his sleeve, grumbling knowing that, while Jumping Edward and his irksome mother had been effective, and admittedly rather fun, the hasty move had expended more chrys than he would have hoped.

Acting more cautiously, Burk stayed at his post and observed the group at a distance. He replaced his oculars, hiding them under the brim of his cap, and kept a close watch, switching the modes on his compass now and then to take readings of his targets while keeping their signatures in close range.

As the hours passed, the clouds invaded the once clear, blue sky, warning of possible inclement weather ahead. Simultaneously, the frequency of car and foot traffic increased, drawing in even more shoppers and would-be diners. Lack of visibility, both from the dreary weather and influx of visitors, forced Burk to displace and maintain a more direct line of sight on his targets.

A short while after taking a new position at the fountain in the middle of the avenue, the threesome started their way across the street at the far end of the avenue. Before long, it started to drizzle, growing to a crescendo of downpouring rain. Passersby rushed in every direction and the sidewalks were abandoned as people fled to the nearest source of shelter. Those at the center avenue lay at the mercy of oncoming traffic, waiting for an opening before tearing off to seek refuge.

Burk watched his targets as they waited in the center avenue, using another setting on his oculars to see through the rain, calculating their probable paths. The female target had stopped scanning the traffic and, Burk noticed, for the third time that day, was glaring right at him.

This one seems rather sharp, he thought, making eye

contact with the female through his oculars. The rain acted as his cover; he Jumped surreptitiously as a group crossed his path to a safe location, turning to see the female staring on before being whisked away by one of her male cohorts. Burk watched them cross the street to the safety of the sidewalk– and while the males dashed into the nearest shop, Burk was not surprised to find that the female had stopped, spun around, and spotted him once again.

The exchange of stares was severed, however, by a mass of shrieking adolescents passing before Burk, jackets held above their heads to shield themselves while seeking refuge from the elements. Burk seized the opportunity and Jumped, reappearing beside a tent stationed across from the store that the male targets had chosen for shelter. Seeing the female target rejoin her male counterparts inside, Burk walked his way around and entered through the back flap.

Inside, a handful of people stood at the front of the tent with arms crossed, shivering where they stood as they stared vacantly through the opening of the tent flap. The rush for cover drew the attention of those inside away from Burk, whose enormous figure had taken up a large amount of space amongst the group. Aiming to remain a sideshow rather than the main attraction, Burk sank himself into the furthest dark corner that the tent offered. He pulled back his sopping sleeve to reveal his compass, scanning the scene to ensure he'd remained unnoticed. After wiping away the damp surface of the device, he dialed in a series of codes, then recovered his forearm with his soaked sleeve.

The compass hummed to life, then let out a low and steady buzz. The occupants of the tent paid no mind, too far away to hear much else than the rain hammering against the canvas above. Burk felt a surge of energy as a prickling sensation pulsed through his body, calming to that of a comforting warmth.

The interface of his oculars faded. A series of icons and images projected and rolled across his field of view, dwindling back towards the center, then vanished, leaving him with a polarized view of the world around him. A glowing red interface popped into existence and Burk's right pupil sequenced, expanding and contracting as it configured itself to interface with his surroundings. The sequencing rolled to a stop, leaving Burk with enhanced vision and a crisp dashboard integrated with his environment.

Curling the fingers on his left hand, Burk squeezed inward towards his palm. A single puff of hot steam shot like tiny cannons from every pore of his body, lifting his clothes from his skin and covering him in a layer of hot air. His cap flew from his head, and he snatched it, saving it from escaping towards the canvas roof. Now dry, he dusted himself off, first batting his cap with his right hand before replacing it on his head, then swiped the front legs of his trousers. He fixed the creases in his shirt, buttoned his coat, and placed his oculars in his front breast pocket.

From the back of the tent, Burk looked past the patrons stationed at the front and zeroed in on the store across the street, spotting the targets he'd been tailing. Similar to the lot in the tent, the group stood soaking and shaking, staring into the rain, waiting for a blue sky to reveal itself.

As he waited for their next move, Burk recalled the face of the female who had caught wind of his presence multiple times that day. Aside from her keen sense of awareness, there seemed to be nothing remarkable about the girl at all. Burk's primary focus had been towards the youngest male in the group, but aside from his sudden appearance earlier that morning, neither he nor the older male had acted in any way worth noting since. Still, he needed to prepare a comprehensive report for the Commission–and Janice–to consider the matter settled, even if it meant getting up close and personal.

As the rain faded and the clouds parted, the tent's temporary refugees dispersed one-by-one. Once the rain died down to a mere whisper, none but Burk and the shopkeeper remained. At that moment, his targets left their chosen sanctuary and slowly moved towards the south end of the row of colorful shops.

Burk exited the back of the tent, moving fast to not lose visual contact with the group. A smart move on his part, as he saw the smallest of them make a sudden dash, tearing down the sidewalk and weaving in and out of foot traffic that had reappeared with a reemergence of clear skies and sunshine.

Behind the tents, Burk jumped towards the south end, positioning himself at a vantage point where he could see where the boy was headed. He took notice of a rainbow-colored building–the glass door branded with the giant head of a cartoonish pink cow with its tongue sticking out to lick a vanilla ice cream cone. It had been eons since Burk had eaten ice cream, but even he knew enough about children to determine that the parlor was likely the boy's intended destination. Observing the pace of the older male and female, Burk further surmised they were in no rush to catch up with the youngest of their group.

Using his Augmented eye, Burk zoomed past the glass doorway of the shop to make out a handful of customers waiting in queue. Through the window near the counter, he saw a single shopkeeper busy at work plunge headfirst into the ice cream cooler with a scoop in hand. Scanning from left to right, a gap in the queue presented itself. A man stood on one side of the gap, squinting up at the shop's menu. On the other, a group of teenage females, all of whom were too busy giggling to pay any proper attention to their place in line.

Popping out of and back into existence, Burk Jumped to occupy the gap in the disorderly queue. Aside from one of the teens shooting Burk a confused look, he had otherwise integrated into the ice cream shop's queue undetected. He glared at the confused teen, who looked down at her feet, choosing to keep to herself rather than question the monstrous figure before her.

From behind, Burk heard the shop door swing open, followed promptly by a bell, which chimed happily to welcome customers as they entered the shop. He turned to see the small boy he had been following. The boy beamed with joy as he looked around with wide eyes and an even wider smile.

Burk was almost jealous at the sight of his elation, wishing that anything in the world could make him just as happy.

As the boy stood, more patrons flooded the shop. Paying the young lad no mind, they hurried past him and into the queue, tripling its length in a matter of seconds. The boy, realizing he never took his place in line, dropped his head in embarrassment and began sauntering to the queue's end.

"Hey there, son," said Burk, causing the boy's ears to perk and look in his direction. "What are you called?"

"Luka," replied the boy timidly.

"Nice to make your acquaintance, Luka," said Burk softly. "I'm terribly sorry, but it looks to me that these foul folks were quick to ignore a gentleman such as yourself to give themselves a leg up in the queue." The guilty parties made themselves look busy, inspecting their surroundings at random, hoping to avoid confrontation.

"Care to join me?" asked Burk.

Luka nodded with renewed enthusiasm, skipping to stand next to Burk in the queue.

"Thanks!" said Luka politely.

"Not a problem, Luka. And how has your day been?" asked Burk, looking down as he towered over him.

"Fine," replied Luka, splitting his attention between answering Burk and looking over the menu hanging above a glass case filled with buckets of ice cream. "I'm here with my brother and my best friend. It's her birthday today!"

"Is it now?" said Burk with notable interest, "and might I ask what birthday she's celebrating?"

"She's celebrating *her* birthday," said Luka matter-of-factly.

"No, no, m' boy," chuckled Burk, "I mean, how old is she today?"

"Oh," said Luka, flushing with embarrassment. "Sixteen, I think." The red of his blushing cheeks faded as Luka burst with excitement, the two having moved to the front of the line. Luka gazed at the ice cream man behind the counter dressed from head to toe in white, topped with a soda jerk hat complete with the branding of a cheerful pink cow next to a tub of ice cream surrounded by a glowing rainbow.

"What'll it be then, gents?" asked the ice cream man. He spoke to them both, but looked at Luka to avoid direct eye contact with Burk.

"Well?" said Burk to Luka. "What'll it be, son?" He saw the smile wiped clean from Luka's face. Luka panicked and felt his pockets, desperate to find some form of payment. Burk, recognizing the situation at hand, put the boy's troubled mind at ease.

"Anything you want," said Burk, "my treat."

Smiling once more, Luka politely asked for a scoop of chocolate ice cream with sprinkles in a waffle cone. Burk relayed Luka's request to the ice cream man, who fulfilled the order. Burk was handed an overflowing waffle cone, which he exchanged for a singular bank note, then met Luka on a bent knee, completing the transaction as he passed the cone off into Luka's hands, which shook with excitement.

"Ah, there must be your compatriots," said Burk, turning to the door to see the male and female targets at the front of the shop. They stood idly by, staring at him shamelessly. Feeling like the main attraction at a carnival show, Burk broke the awkward tension by ushering Luka along to his friends. Failing to break their gaze, he coughed as he stood, snapping the onlookers out of their trance.

With his targets assembled, Burk seized the opportunity to keep their attention and gather as much intel as possible. He initiated small talk, simultaneously conducting full body scans of each of them in search of any oddities that could account for the source of the ripple. Burk completed Luka's scan quickly, doing so before the older male and female dismissed Luka to the outdoor dining area. The result was both a relief and a disappointment to Burk. Luka's readings were immaterial across the board, which meant he had cleared one potential target, but still had not identified the cause of the ripple.

"Apologies, I've had the pleasure of meeting young Luka, but I haven't gotten your names," said Burk, biding his time to complete another scan.

"Sorry, I'm Addy. This is my friend, Eli."

"Yes, Eli Smith," he said, reaching out for a handshake. "Luka is my younger brother."

Burk felt his heart skip a beat, but continued to focus on

the task at hand. "Ah," he said, grasping Eli by the hand and taking considerably more time than normal to release his grip. He held his gaze on Eli, allowing him to conduct a far more intricate scan. His interface lit up, stating that Eli had over a fifty percent chance of being suited for Augmentation, but found no sign that he had transitioned or was able to use his inherent abilities in any capacity. "Two gentlemen, I see. Your parents must be very proud."

Burk finished his statement and released Eli from his grip. He was now running on autopilot, his attention taken by a sea of swirling thoughts. He stood half suspended in disbelief and was struggling to register what he had heard. Assuming, of course, he had heard them correctly. If they were truly called by the names they said–Addy, Eli, and Luka–it would certainly be a wild coincidence, he thought. He racked his brain, trying to make sense of it all, struggling to connect the dots. Those names had triggered something deep in his memory. A feeling–one he had long ago suppressed–had resurfaced, leaving him to rediscover the emptiness inside him, tangled in a web of anger, frustration, and confusion.

"I see you don't have any ice cream...You don't seem to be very wet..." said Addy decisively. Despite the shell-shock, Burk had enough remaining wit to gather that Addy had started to interrogate him. Burk, who was able to convey calm and order in the stormiest of weathers, responded to her inquiries without issue. He made up what he figured to be reasonable responses as he went along, focusing his efforts on remaining neutral as his mind continued to stir. But he could only keep the charade up for so long. His inner thoughts overshadowed his ability to focus on the conversation. He needed a moment alone. A moment to regroup. He needed to get away from Addy and Eli and Luka.

"Well, I must be off," said Burk hastily, unsure as to the last words Addy and Eli had said. "It was very lovely to meet the both of you. I do hope that our paths cross again."

13.
STEP 2A: DON'T PANIC

What just happened? Burk pondered shakily. He had left the ice cream parlor and taken solace on a recently vacated bench. The three previous occupants had scurried off, no doubt frightened at the sight of Burk as he stormed in their direction. On the outside, Burk was as stiff as a board. On the inside, he was trembling.

Addy, Eli, and Luka...he repeated the names over and over again in his head. *How long had it been since those names held meaning to him? Twenty-fifty-one hundred annos?* Burk contemplated tirelessly. Years of traveling through time had made the act of recalling distant memories a cumbersome and murky task. When the 'when' of life's path stops being linear, it's tough to keep everything else straight.

It doesn't matter how long it's been. If that lot is who they say-who they might be-that means everything...it means that she isn't truly lost. It means there could be a way for me to save her.

Burk sat motionless on the bench, trying to look as though he belonged right where he was. He remained calm despite himself. The battle in his head waged on.

Does it now? Tell me, how many times have we been down this road?

Burk strained as he tried to guess how much time he had wasted hunting down answers to impossible questions. The leads he discovered, the trouble he caused, and the overwhelming, inevitable feeling of misery that he found waiting for him as he traveled down bitter paths that led to death, despair, and dead ends.

So, you'll just give up then, eh? That's what you do now?

No. A quitter, Burk was not. But he had to move on. Everyone has to move on, eventually. He'd hardened himself up to numb the pain he'd experienced over the years, and he knew now that if he embarked on this journey, dared to go down another road riding the faintest glimmer of hope, taking a path that might lead him to yet another dead end, it would rip him apart all over.

Say her name then.

Burk tried to recall her name. Hell, he didn't need to try; he knew it. It was right there for the taking. He could reach out and grab it if he wanted. But he'd done that too many times before. The dark had cast out the light, and it was clear to him that the path was likely to lead to nowhere. He wasn't willing to trek it, to open any more wounds. Those he had were already too much to handle.

Coward.

Burk huffed quietly and got to his feet. Regardless of his feelings, there was still a job to be done, and he had no ambivalence about seeing it to fruition. He turned back towards the ice cream parlor, scanning as he moved to find Addy, Eli, and Luka. He repositioned himself at the back of the shop, standing a head above a crowd of gawkers that had grouped together nearby.

Turning his oculars back on, Burk spotted Addy, Eli, and Luka on the ice cream parlor's patio. The three seemed to be engaged in an unpleasant conversation with a gangly woman in all white and a fat little lad who seemed to have been stuffed inside a small, stain ridden shirt. Absorbed in his own thoughts and self-pity only a moment ago, Burk had missed the initial point when the groups had engaged with one another. He was surprised to find them in a tiff of sorts, which had already escalated to the point where the woman appeared ready to become physical with Addy. Burk watched as the woman in white raised her hand and struck Addy in the chest. Addy was quick to deflect, thrusting the woman's hand away in self-defense.

The altercation shifted from physical violence to panicked shouting. Little by little, the noise attracted more-and-more passersby, forming a crowd that wrung its way around the patio to observe the scene. This was of no consequence to Burk, who stood well above the tallest member of the crowd.

Reverting to his oculars, he cycled through its settings and took readings once more. He had been remiss in completing an evaluation of Addy; surely, the mounting pressure caused by the group's current predicament would be enough to elicit a noteworthy response if any of them were capable of producing one.

Staring into the void with no results, Burk switched his settings to thermal. A new male figure crossed his line of sight to join the commotion on the patio, running first to the aid of the bellowing woman. Burk could hear murmurs from gawkers as they deliberated around the scene–their whispers growing into open and shameless accusations directed at his targets. Some of the bolder onlookers shouted out their grievances towards Addy, Eli, and Luka, singling them out as the cause of all the commotion. Burk took his time to inspect each member of the threesome, studying every observable variable his tools would allow. First was Luka, who gave off ordinary readings in all regards (aside from thermal, which showed a distinct ring of purple around his lips). Next came Eli's readings, which, by all accounts, were equally ordinary; perhaps even less astounding than earlier, with Eli's probability for Augmentation dropping below fifty percent.

Burk turned to Addy and prepared to scan. He felt his heart flutter, then drum against his chest. While Addy's body temperature was normal, her figure was surrounded at the waist by an oblong, bulbous glow, burning so ferociously white that Burk was forced to avoid viewing it through his organic eye. His augmented eye continued to work, but only at half its normal ability. The view before him became fuzzy, but allowed him to discern the edges of a glowing mass that grew indiscriminately, covering the area where Addy once stood. Another moment passed before Burk transitioned his optics, readying himself to scan for signs of chrys. Readying himself for what he feared might come next.

Nothing.

Burk checked the settings on his oculars in validation. Yes, they were correct; yes, he was scanning for chrys; yes, he had indeed recorded what seemed to be an immense anomalous glow, but he was now gazing into a void. He changed the setting on his oculars back to thermal–the angelic orb having been extinguished–keeping Burk from conducting any further analysis. In its wake, a signature of elevated heat floated in the air like a mist, fading into two exclusive orbs, twinkling like rubies near Addy's center and the location of the once fiery white globe. The crimson orbs traversed the thermal gradient–from red to yellow to green–and settled down before taking on a shade of oceanic blue.

Addy, much like her companions, had become completely ordinary once again.

* * *

Burk moved stealthily under the cover of the woods, traveling parallel to a covered highway that was being traversed by the truck that carried Addy, Eli, and Luka. When the vehicle turned onto a secluded dirt road, Burk recognized the sole path that would lead him back to the farmstead and to Sky. He overtook the truck with caution, Jumping a great distance to remain hidden as he raced to beat the group back to their intended destination.

In miraculous time, Burk found himself opposite the fence enclosing the farmstead and prowled along the tree line. Turning on his oculars, he spotted a twinkling purple mass in the shape of a crooked L that had been pushed on its side in the distance. The mass was immobile, stationed amid a mess of gray that outlined a hodgepodge of downed trees.

Burk neared the mass and reverted his oculars back to normal. Unsurprised, but disappointed all the same, he identified the source of the blob: Sky. The recruit sat with his arms crossed, back propped against a tree stump; his lower torso curved in an uncomfortable-looking position towards the damp soil, connected to legs that splayed and extended into the forest while his oculars rested half on his face. His mouth sat wide open, bringing with it a song of shallow, intermittent snoring.

With a groan and accompanying eye roll, Burk gave his recruit a swift kick to the leg.

"Huh–I–who," mumbled a now conscious Sky, arms flailing and head bobbing back and forth.

"Well, good morning, princess. Have ourselves a nice bit of kip, did we?"

"Oh," said Sky, getting to his feet and brushing off the leaves that had fallen on him while he slept. "Burk–I, well, there isn't a whole hell of a lot going on here. Kind of hard to stay alert when you haven't given me a lot to do. Where the hell have you been for so long, anyway?"

"First off, I'll be the one asking the questions here, son, so mind yourself in that regard," said Burk, taking a knee behind a downed tree. "As for your snide retort, you should know that the primary characteristic of any stakeout is that nothing happens for the vast majority of it. That's part of the job, son–better get used to it.

Sky stretched and shook off his post-nap fatigue while Burk continued.

"You'll find that the second key component of a stakeout is that the important bits seem to happen all at once when you least expect it. Let's hope you didn't end up missing out during what I'm sure was not at all a short break." Burk rummaged through his reclaimed pack and pulled out a long, metallic canteen.

"As for where I've been," continued Burk, stopping momentarily to take a pull of water from his container. "Well, even you should be smart enough to deduce that I've been tailing our three new friends. But more on that later. Do you mind explaining why you turned your compass off while I was gone?"

"Why does that matter? And how did you know?" asked Sky curtly.

"Had it been on, I could've located your coordinates and Jumped right back to your location," said Burk, pulling small silver bags from his larger pack. "So, you'll have no one to thank but yourself for the added boredom. Now, would you mind answering my questions or should I find some equally uninteresting task for you to complete instead?"

"I didn't want to waste the energy," said Sky, scowling. "After you left to follow the truck, the older woman in the house on the left and the guy from the house on the right had a chat outside. The woman got a bit heated, but nothing really happened for a while after that. The old bat and her dog left at some point but that was ages ago–you told me not to engage, so I stayed behind to watch the guy, but he hasn't done much other than smoke and drink. Hasn't even left the same room since he went back inside, so I thought I'd be resourceful and put my compass to sleep to save the chrys until I needed it."

Burk thought about Sky's reasoning and, to their collective amazement, seemed to agree with his approach. "Fair enough," he said.

"Aside from the shuteye, which I'm willing to overlook at the moment," continued Burk as he handed Sky an open bag of rations, "Did you see anything else? Overhear anything that the other two may have spoken about?"

"Yeah, I did actually—"

The front door of the rightmost house flew open. A man with peppered hair wearing a grimy tank top and tattered jeans stumbled through it. A half-crumbled cigarette dangled between the man's lips. In his right hand, he gripped the handle of a half-gallon of whiskey. Rebounding from his floundering entrance, the man grasped a chair from the front porch of the house, yanked it down the front set of stairs, dragged it through the mud, stopped at a spot between the two houses, and flopped down on top of it.

Sky and Burk observed the man in silence, taking cover behind a wooded brush. They watched as he took a long pull from his whiskey bottle before struggling to light his cigarette, dropping his flame multiple times in the failed attempt. Sky and Burk exchanged a look, agreeing without words that the target before them was unaware of their presence and, even if he were, would prove to be a threat to no one but himself.

They resumed consuming their rations as Burk recalled the events of his day in town, conveniently leaving out any information that might pique Sky's interest and prompt further discussion or bothersome questions.

"Well, that'll be that then," said Burk, finishing his rations and folding the empty silver pouch before placing it neatly back in his bag. "Once the truck gets back, we'll take one last reading here, then we'll start our journey back to the Present."

"Wha'?" spluttered Sky, choking down a mouthful of rations. "We came all the way here for nothing? What the hell was the point? We didn't even find the source of the cripple—"

"Ripple," Burk corrected him.

"Ripple, sure, whatever. Are you sure it's not the children? They seem to be the only possibility at this point," said Sky hastily.

"Don't get hasty," said Burk, fingering through the manila

folder in his bag. "I vetted those three thoroughly and there's nothing we need to worry about from that lot. We'll have to make a stop between outposts on the way back. Maybe more, depending on how much chrys they've managed to hole up for weary travelers like us. I'm sure one of those stops is bound to be of more interest than what we've been tasked to do here. That's what you want, isn't it?"

Sky gaped at Burk, looking flummoxed. Burk sensed the recruit's confusion. *Perhaps I'm being too kind to the boy*, he thought. But before Burk could quash Sky's apparent concerns or Sky could pose further inquiry, their collective attention was stolen away by the grating sounds of a truck struggling down the dirt road in their direction.

"Oh, by the way," said Sky, fumbling with the interface of his compass. "I heard the name of the other guy from the woman. She called him Magnus, I think. Couldn't make out her name, though. Might've been Providence or something like that–I dunno."

Sky continued toying with his monitor. He was too busy to notice that Burk's marred face had become devoid of color, transforming him from a monstrous ogre to a pale ghost.

14.
THE INCIDENT

Addy slept with her head rested on her right shoulder, rattling around as the truck struggled against loose gravel and dirt. A soft spot in the road gave in to the weight of the truck's front tire, jerking the vehicle forward and Addy along with it, causing her to wake with an alarming gasp.

"Jesus!" exclaimed Eli. "You alright, Ads?" Neither the dip in the road nor Eli's loud inquiries had affected Luka, who stayed fast asleep, cozying up even closer to Addy's side.

"I'm...fine," said Addy with a pause as the sensation of falling subsided. Silence lingered between them, taking up space in the already cramped truck cab.

"Sorry about today," said Eli, finally cracking under the pressure of the long and silent ride.

"It's fine. Don't worry about it," said Addy curtly.

"You say that, but I know you, Ads. I was just trying to do what's best," said Eli.

"Sure–I know," said Addy unconvincingly.

"C'mon now, you know I was! What would've happened if Guinevere had pressed charges, hmm? I mean, don't get me wrong, I would've had your back either way. Trust me when I say, I know you can handle yourself, but think about it. You really want to waste your time with that prat in court? How would it look to the academy if you were involved in something like that?"

"Assuming I get in," muttered Addy.

"You're brilliant, Ads," he assured her. "No way you don't get in–front of the line, I reckon. I mean, you may need to work on that temper of yours a bit before we ship you off, but you look excellent on paper," grinned Eli.

"Oh hah-hah," replied Addy whimsically.

"Just don't forget about us when you're all successful and rich and whatnot while I'm out toiling away in the fields trudging on," said Eli, trying to keep the mood light.

"Why would you say that?" asked Addy.

"I'm only joking!" replied Eli in a trice, wishing he could take it back at the realization his witty remark had had the opposite effect of his intentions.

"I don't want to leave any of you! The only reason I applied in the first place is because you and Prue kept insisting that I had to," said Addy.

"Addy, I—"

"And I'll remind you that the *only* reason I don't work the fields as much as you do these days is because you won't let me!" she explained. Her elevated tone caused Luka to stir next to her in his sleep. Addy took no notice and continued mockingly, parroting Eli's voice. "*You've got to study, Ad's. You're too smart, Ad's. Get out of this godforsaken country, Ad's. Go out and live your dream, Ads.*"

"Excuse me for trying to help you do more with your life than spend it on a bloody farm," said Eli.

"Well, what if that's what I want? What if being with you, and Luka, and Prue, wherever that may be, is enough for me? Have you ever considered that?"

"We'll always be here for you, Ads," said Eli calmly, circumventing his frustration. "But we both know your ambitions are well beyond that. Can you honestly say you'd be happy doing the same thing out here every day? That you wouldn't resent us–not even a little–for not pushing you to try? I know I would."

"Why don't *you* do it then?" said Addy curtly.

"That's different and you know it," sighed Eli. "I've got to watch over Luka. There's no way he can grow up in that house with Magnus all on his own."

"Yeah? And who's going to watch over the two of you if I'm gone?" asked Addy.

"That's easy. I take care of Eli, and we leave Prue and Mico to keep a close eye on Magnus. He'd be a fool to step out of line 'round those two," said Eli.

"But—"

Eli cursed without warning, startling Addy and causing Luka to wake up. Eli stared wide eyed out the front windshield as Addy faced forward, their distant farmstead coming into view more clearly. She eventually realized, much to her dismay, why Eli was so upset: Magnus. The boys' father sat on a rocking chair between the two homes, surrounded by partially smoked cigarettes and holding a half-empty whiskey jug.

"Where are we?" asked Luka drowsily.

"We're almost home," Addy replied, not giving Luka her full attention as she mentally prepared herself, uncertain of what was to come. She hoped that Prue and Mico would show themselves and cast her worries aside. Her hope diminished with each passing second, fizzling away as they crossed the threshold of the farmstead's drive.

Eli gripped the steering wheel, white knuckled and wide eyed as the truck rumbled up the drive. He cautiously drove into the dusty driveway, keeping his head down to avoid his father's glare. He could only see him from the corner of his eye and didn't dare to make eye contact. The vehicle rolled forward. A truck length between them and Magnus, Eli shifted the gear into park, pulled the keys from the ignition, and handed them furtively to Addy.

"Can you take Luka inside? And hide these?" Eli whispered

to Addy, who simply nodded, watching as Magnus took a swig from his oversized jug. Only a portion of the jug's contents found its way into his mouth while the rest drooled down the sides of his face and neck before being absorbed by his musty tank top. Magnus lowered the jug and, using his forearm, sloppily wiped the excess dribble from his face. He then set the jug in the dirt, struggled to his feet, and made his way to the truck's driver side door, rapping repeatedly on the window.

Eli opened the door of the truck. Addy grasped Luka by the arm, yanking him from the vehicle as delicately and quickly as she could before ushering the perplexed child towards her house. With each step, she hoped Prue and Mico would reveal themselves to help, and to put a stop to the trouble that was bound to unfold.

"I want to see dad," whined Luka.

"In a bit, Luka, he's not feeling well right now, but don't worry. Eli and I will get him sorted and you can see him after," said Addy, scooting Luka along while listening intently to the conversation behind her.

"Wha'? You na' goin' to let me see ma' own son, then?" drawled Magnus.

"It's best he doesn't see you like this," said Eli delicately.

"And who said–*who said,* you could take ma' truck? Where'd you ge' off?" said Magnus.

"Magnus, please. Do we really have to do this today?" asked Eli.

"Magnus, pfft–if you'll not be callin' me dah', then you—" paused Magnus, taking in a deep breath.

"What?" asked Eli.

"Then you bett'r be callin' me, sir! Understood?"

Addy opened her front door and peered inside the house. She called out for Prue and Mico, holding her breath, hoping they would reply. Calling out once more, Addy's heart sank. The house sat vacant, and her body flushed with anxiety as a harsh reality set in. Magnus was drunk and seemed to be headed down a warpath. She would need to deal with him without the help of her grandmother or trusty companion to keep him at bay.

"Luka, stay here, okay? I'll be back with your brother in a minute," said Addy, tossing the keys into a planter near the door as she escorted Luka to a worn leather armchair in the living room. Luka plopped down and comforted himself in the chair. Feet dangling, he casually swung his legs and looked up at Addy, giving her a subtle nod. Addy forced a grin and nodded back. She then turned on her heel, opened the front door, and started towards Eli, Magnus, and the sounds of their unyielding exchange.

"You are drunk, *sir*. Please, let's get you inside," said Eli indignantly.

"Don't use that tone with me, *boy*," scolded Magnus, waspishness getting the better of him. "Don' you walk 'way from me when I'm talkin' to you!"

"I'm not going anywhere," said Eli, passing Magnus to meet Addy at the edge of the drive.

Addy took her place next to Eli, taking in Magnus' gorilla-like figure as he spun to face them. Inebriated as Magnus may have been, Addy knew from experience that the man was still a force to be reckoned with. And while she felt more than capable of standing up to him in her own defense, it wouldn't be her taking the brunt of the consequences. She reluctantly admitted that, for the sake of her friends, she would have to take a note out of Eli's book and adopt a more passive approach.

Magnus caught Addy's eyes. He straightened himself up, seeming to regain his composure in an instant.

"Where are my keys?" asked Magnus, setting back his broad shoulders.

"Sorry, Mr. Smith. Haven't a clue," said Addy.

"Adelynne. Give me the keys," commanded Magnus, though rather dejectedly.

"I assure you, I don't have them," she said sensibly.

"Fine," said Magnus, glaring at Addy. "Then where's my son?"

"You can see him after you sober up," said Eli.

"I wasn't talking to you," said Magnus coldly.

"He's right, Mr. Smith," vouched Addy. "Why do you want to see him, anyway?"

"I don't see how that's any o' your concern," asserted Magnus.

"Anything to do with the well-being of Luka and Eli, I consider my concern," insisted Addy.

"Now come on, let's not—" started Eli.

"Ah, yes. Still letting women fight your battles for you, I see," laughed Magnus.

"Eli is perfectly capable of defending himself," retorted Addy quickly.

"Not helping, Ads," groaned Eli under his breath.

"I can see 'at, *Adelynne.* And what I can see now is that I was wrong before. No son o' mine would be so keen to let a woman come to his aid," snarled Magnus. "No son of mine at all," he concluded, spitting at Eli's feet before looking at the boy in contempt.

Eli vacillated between the spit at his feet and Magnus' harsh words. Magnus took a step forward.

"Nothing to say, eh? Goin' to let these bitches do 'erything for you?" said Magnus, taking another step.

Stay calm, thought Addy, feeling her insides boil, resisting the urge to lash out in her defense.

"That's wha' I thought. Some son of mine you are—"

"Some father you are," said Eli, quivering. "Wasting away your days piss drunk. It's because of us you even have the means to buy that shite. If it wasn't for us–wasn't for Addy and Prue," he nodded towards Addy with gratitude. "You wouldn't have a pot to piss in," continued Eli with growing confidence, "so don't talk to me about using women to fight my battles, old man, because the way I see it, everyone here has been doing that on your behalf for years."

Magnus huffed and strutted past the duo, dropping his shoulder as he crossed paths with Eli and knocking him off balance. Addy grabbed Eli's arm at the last second to keep him from falling.

"Mr. Smith, do not go in there," declared Addy.

"I don't need permission from either of you," growled Magnus. "And while we're at it, I don't need anything from you or 'at old bag, Prue," Magnus said, piling on a few crude nicknames for Addy and her grandmother. Names that, if Luka were present to hear, would have raised a lot of uncomfortable questions.

You wouldn't have the guts to say any of this if Prue were here, thought Addy, biting her tongue.

"You know, it just dawned on me," yelled Eli in Magnus' direction. "If this is how you really feel about women, then it's no wonder why mom up and left."

Magnus stopped dead in his tracks.

"Yeah, that must've been it," surmised Eli. "You won't talk about her. Won't speak about what happened. I always blamed myself, but it's clear to me now why she did it. It was *your* fault. Not mine. Not Luka's. *Yours.* Look at you, attacking the people that care about you. That's why she left, didn't she? Because of you! You're the reason we haven't got a mother!"

What happened next would change the very nature of reality, as they all knew it.

By the time the word "mother" had escaped Eli's mouth, Magnus had wrapped one of his burly paws around Eli's throat, shoving Addy aside in the process to reach him. Addy fell to her knees and looked up in disbelief. Her feeling of pride towards Eli was short-lived as she tried to come to grips with the situation unfolding before her. She watched on, twisted into a state of shock, as Magnus lifted Eli into the air with extraordinary ease; Eli writhed under Magnus' grip, kicking his feet and floundering like a fish gasping for air, clawing at his captor's wrist, desperate to free himself. Then, in a remarkable display of strength, Magnus cocked his arm back with Eli firmly in his grasp and hurdled the young man through the air. Eli slammed into the side door of the truck, crumbling to the dirt like a rag doll.

"Eli!" shrieked Luka, escaping the confines of the house to rush to his brother's aid. Hearing the boy's cries brought Addy back to reality. From her knees, she lunged and grabbed Luka by the arm at the last second. She pulled him into her chest, fighting to keep a tight hold on the wriggling boy to protect him from the same fate as his brother.

"Mr. Smith, please stop!" cried Addy, her eyes pooling with tears and frustration, torn between letting Luka go to help Eli and keeping him safely at her side. Magnus ignored her cries and pursued Eli, who stood pitifully keeled over at the waist. Addy and Luka yelled out, pleading for Magnus to end his rampage.

"Dad! Dad, please, no!" cried Luka.

"Magnus, stop it! Let him go!" yelled Addy.

They watched in horror as Magnus clutched Eli by the hairs of his slouched head. He yanked Eli upward to look him in the eye; Eli returned the gesture, smiling at Magnus with a bloody grin. Then, gravity on his side, Eli fell back and kicked upward with all his might, aiming for the only area with the potential to bring his raging father to his knees. But Magnus was ready, and his free hand caught Eli by the shin as though it had been waiting there to meet it all along. He held Eli in the air like a contorted marionette; Eli looked up in astonishment before being thrust forcefully against the side door of the truck once more.

Even for Magnus, things had gone too far. Addy knew this, but she was still having trouble believing what she was seeing. It was too much, and she thought of Luka and Eli, and how to keep them safe, and how it was so unfair. *If I hadn't pushed Eli, none of this would be happening*, she thought. Her frustration churned itself into a ball in her chest and tears streaked freely from her eyes. She was useless, unable to protect herself, unable to protect her friends all over again. Despair took hold–her grip on Luka gave way.

Luka's relentless squirming paid off for the boy. Taking advantage of the opportunity, he broke free from Addy and sprinted towards his battered brother. The boy grew nearer to Magnus, and Addy's momentary lapse weighed on her heavily. The feelings of frustration and guilt in her chest transformed. She felt her blood boil and shot upright. Seething with anger, she marched forward with purpose, each step strengthening and reviving her bold tendencies.

Ahead, Eli sought refuge and fled under the truck, crawling frantically to reach the green grass on the other side. Magnus dropped to his knees and thrust himself forward, catching Eli by the heel while dodging attempted kicks to the face. Eli's legs stiffened under the weight of Magnus. Unable to move, he resorted to digging his claws into the dirt, holding the Earth in desperation to avoid being pulled back. With a jerk, Eli found himself out from under the truck, flailing about wildly, struggling against great odds to keep Magnus at bay.

His efforts were to no avail, and Eli was overtaken with startling ease. Magnus, unscathed, seized Eli by the collar and yanked the tired young man towards him, cocking his other arm back to strike. But he was caught off balance; Luka took hold of Magnus at the elbow, clinging to him for dear life. Magnus staggered backwards, releasing Eli and using his free arm to prevent himself from falling. He began flapping his arms, twisting and turning to undermine Luka's unyielding grip and fling him away. Luka cried out, begging Magnus to leave his brother alone.

Depleted, but unwilling to abandon his brother, Eli rejoined the scuffle and struck Magnus from behind. Magnus ignored the blow entirely, treating Eli like a bothersome fly, easily brushing him aside. Luka responded to his brother's defeat with a jarring battle-cry, opening his jaws wide and clamping down on his father's elbow. Magnus yelped; the sting of the boy's sharp teeth sank in. Magnus growled like a hound as he battled against his youngest son to regain control. He found an opening and snatched Luka by the ankle, wrenching the courageous boy from his vice-like grip, then raised him in the air like a freshly caught fish.

Luka glared defiantly at the upturned face of his father. Magnus had never dared to strike his youngest son before, but in that instant, and without hesitation, he decided Luka would need to be punished.

Turning his palm outward, Magnus cocked his hand back once again, ready to deal the boy an unforgettable blow. Luka slammed his eyes shut and winced, bracing himself for the inevitable impact. Magnus swung his arm forward towards Luka–experiencing an immediate feeling of sobering regret–not for Luka's sake, but for his own.

Magnus' eyes widened in terror. Addy had suddenly manifested before him, placing herself between Magnus and Luka; her face drawn with unquantifiable scorn, her stature the embodiment of wrath itself, devoid of color or warmth. But it was too late to change course. Magnus braced for impact as his hand, the one meant for Luka, bore down on Addy.

Addy, beside herself physically and mentally, did not feel the sting of Magnus' hand. Instead, she felt an overwhelming heat grow from the anger that had built inside her. And for a moment, she felt as if she was watching everything from outside of her own body. She looked down curiously at the sight–her hair floated angelically, her skin radiant and glowing. A scintillating light undulated from her center. She felt calm as the pace of her surroundings slowed to a stop. She gazed around at her environment, captivated by the stillness.

The calm subsided as a blinding white light poured outward from Addy's core. The light expanded, exploding into a colossal white globe that rippled across the countryside. She gazed on through the light, watching in awe as Magnus flew back and began tumbling through the air. She turned her attention to Eli and Luka, overcome with relief at the sight of her friends lying safely beside her, unharmed by the blast.

The rippling of light fluttered and came to a halt. Addy looked down at her feet, reunited with her body once again. Her overwhelming anger subsided, and she shivered. She felt cold and faint, far from the comfortable feeling of warmth that had overcome her moments prior. Her vision blurred, and she staggered forward, reaching out towards Eli and Luka. She took one step forward and found herself too exhausted to attempt another. She surveyed the carnage before her and spotted Magnus, collapsed and unconscious, away from the rest of the group.

Addy let out a sigh of relief and then, succumbing to fatigue, let herself fall into a void of complete darkness.

EPILOGUE

Atop the highest tower at an undisclosed Lookout Commission facility, two young adult males sat before a sprawling control panel. Each man sat in silence with an enormous set of headphones atop their heads and over their ears that hummed a dull tone. They stared at a large monitor at the front of the room, which displayed a large circle at the center that took up most of the space on the floating screen. Sizeable, yet notably smaller circles, surrounded the largest circle on each side. To the untrained eye, it appeared as if someone had drawn the outer edges of the circles with a solid line. However, when the image was enhanced, the outer edges appeared to vibrate.

Brett, who sat on the right side of the control panel, took off his headphones and nudged his research partner, Reginald, who sat on his left. Reginald slid a singular headphone off his right ear and turned to face Brett.

"Reginald, dude," said Brett, "I have a question for you."

"What is it, Brett?" sighed Reginald.

"Just hear me out for a second. Have you ever asked yourself why we wear lab coats? It's not like we work with chemicals and shit. We literally work on computers all day."

"Thank you, Brett. Your commentary, as always, is most appreciated." Reginald motioned to put his headphones back on, but Brett interrupted him and kept going.

"Think about it. How'd we even get the lab coats? Do you remember getting one? I just remember one day, I'd started wearing one, and I can't remember why or where it even came from."

Reginald, realizing that Brett had more questions than he would have hoped, removed his headphones and placed them on the control panel.

"I wear mine because I happen to like it, thank you very much," said Reginald.

"But, dude, like, why? Why do you like wearing it? And when? Do you remember when you even started wearing the thing every day?"

"Listen here, chap. I know we've only worked together for a short while now, but I view myself as a rather excellent judge of a man's character, and I've formed an initial assessment of yours. What are my conclusions, you ask? Foremost, I've surmised that your sole purpose for being here stems from your unhealthy intrigue with our boss, Dr. Schafer. Further, I've deduced that you, just like his followers, wore the lab coat in an attempt to be seen as a member of his trusted inner circle. I'll also add, just to be very clear about that matter, that I am not, in fact, a *dude* as you say. I'm a scientist and an honest gentleman, so any statements you make to me that begin in any other fashion, I'll consider null and void from here on out."

"Dude, first of all, rude," said Brett. "Second, *dude* is a term of endearment, okay? Also, you have got to stop talking like that. Don't get me wrong, my guy, the formal talk is dashing and all, you being all proper like and whatnot. *Oh, look at me govna', I'm a man of science, innit? Chip, chip, cheerio lads!* Listen, all I'm saying is, sometimes, it's a lot. We're going to be working together for a while, so I'm going to need you to slow your roll and chill the eff out. Also, all that said, I'm sorry if me calling you dude genuinely hurts your feelings, so I'm totally down to call you by whatever you want."

"*Beep.*" A singular and subtle sound emits from the men's headphones, which neither of them notice.

"Ah, yes. I see now that I've misjudged you," replied Reginald. "A rarity, to be sure, but I sincerely apologize for that, chap. I rescind my original conclusions and offer a revised alternative. To put it plainly, there's no way a man with such misgivings in the way of common parlance would ever think himself in the running for the favor of Dr. Schafer. And I'll have you know that in terms of preferences, mine would be that you do not speak to me in such a way, you Pasty rodent!"

"*Beep. Beep.*" The headphones produce two more subtle and successive beeps.

"Dude, sir, bro, senior—whatever the hell you prefer. Again, *rude.* Also, just because I don't talk like you doesn't mean I don't understand you, m'kay? Guess what? No one talks like that. Guess what else? My implants? They help me understand every known language in the Past and Present...and guess what, my guy? The way you talk makes it sound like you've got a stick up your arse in every one of them."

"*Beep. Beep. Beep.*"

"Well, I dare say, I never expected an outburst from a man in a position of such authority as yourself. This personal attack on my way of speaking is an affront to my character, and one that I find to be utterly outlandish!"

"*Beep. Beep. Beep. Beep.*"

"Holy shit, dude, how? How's it possible that your speech not only got worse, but you also landed on being a hypocrite as well? The timing, the poetry, it's...", paused Brett, taking a moment to kiss his pinched fingers and thrust them forward. "*C'est magnifique.*"

"*Beep. Beep. Beep. Beep. Beep.*"

"Good heavens! I daresay there's no need to fly into a bate and make such accusations—"

"God," sighed Brett. "Dude, I can't. Just please stop speaking."

The men stop talking and silence fills the air between them.

"*Beep.*"

"I say," said Reginald, "did you hear—"

"*BEEP-BEEP-BEEP-BEEP-BEEP-BEEEEE...*"

The men threw their headphones back on and looked at the front monitor. The outer edges of the largest circle on the screen pulsed violently as a loud and steady tone echoed in their ears. Reginald frantically typed on the control panel, zooming in on the edge of the visibly pulsing circle, and gasped.

"*...EEEEEEEEEEEEP. Beep.*"

Silence fell between them once more.

"So...who's gonna be the one to tell Dr. Schafer the Timeline's frozen?" asked Brett.

Reginald paused, extended the pointer finger on his right hand, and positioned it directly at the tip of his nose.

"Not it."

Z.S. JOSEPH

AUTHOR'S NOTE

Thank you so much for reading Part 1 of The Last Arcadian. It's been a long journey to get to this point, publishing Part 1, and there's still so much more of the story left to tell. In fact, we've only just begun. I'm sure you have a lot of questions, and I'm eager to share more of the story with you as quickly as possible to answer them. In the meantime, here are some answers to questions I've gotten from friends, family, and early readers about the book.

Why did you only publish Part 1?

I had the very beginnings of an idea for what turned into The Last Arcadian somewhere around the time I graduated college and had just started my professional career. That was almost a decade ago. While I'm not planning to take as long to publish part 2, life only gives us so much time in a day. I love this story, and I really hope you enjoyed reading about the first bit of it. That's why I published part 1: To share it with you and get your feedback, learn how to publish a book (and become better at doing it to bring you the story faster), and continue to share more parts of the story as its ready.

How many parts of the book The Last Arcadian are there?

Three. The Last Arcadian, Parts 1-3, is expected to come together as the first book in a multi-book series.

When can we expect Part 2?

Part 2 is already in production, and I'm doing as much as I can to get the rest of the story to you as fast as I can. That said, I also want to give readers the best content possible while remaining true to the story, characters, and world that I've built around it. That, along with my personal and professional commitments, means things will take some time. While I can't set any expectations at the moment, what I can say is that the more the story gets read and shared with others, the more it'll help to speed up the development and release of future content.

What are some of the themes of the story?

The nature of reality, the concept of free will, finding one's purpose, dealing with adversity and existential crisis, making tough and at times impossible decisions and their impact. Those are just a few examples. One of the many things that continues to fascinate me is how little we know about the universe, and how our understanding of it changes at scale, which has tremendous implications for the notion of free will. Each character's understanding of free will, and how that impacts the decisions they make, is one of the major themes explored throughout.

Can I share my feedback about the book with you?

Yes, please! The more the merrier. I'm eager to get your feedback–the good, bad, and ugly–and will read every single review you share on Amazon. If you enjoyed the story, and want to share it with others, then posting a review is one of the best ways to bring it to a wider audience.

Anyone you want to thank?

Thank you, reader, for investing your time, energy, and hard-earned dollars into this story. It's not lost on me that we live in a world with constant access to immeasurable content at your disposal. Whether you loved it, liked it, felt indifferent, or hated it, your investment of time and attention into reading this book means a lot to me. Also, a big thank you to my editor, Alayna Simone, book cover artist, Parker Nugent, and website designer, Sameer Kelkar. I can't thank the three of you enough for all your perspectives, help, and support...and for listening to me go on endless rambles about this story and everything I want to do with it.

How can I stay connected with future publications?

You can visit my website: zsjoseph.com. And you can follow me on Twitter: @zsjoseph_

Made in the USA
Middletown, DE
03 September 2024

59620415R00094